UNFORGETTABLE VALENTINE

Works By Stella Williams

Paranormal Romance

Maura's Men
Suspenseful Vampire Trilogy
Xander's Claim
Claude's Conquest
Shane's Redemption

Secret of Ceres
Magical Romance, Mystery, and Intrigue
Ferocious
Dauntless
Earnest
Zenith - Coming Summer 2021

Langsmith Shifters
Alpha Shifter Shorts
Coy Wolf
A Night Divine
Bird of Prey

Bloodlines
Vampire-Alien Hotties On A Mission for Love
His Soul To Keep

Contemporary Romance
Fun & Seductive
Felling Bechet -Fall 2021
Unforgettable Valentine

Unforgettable Valentine

Print ISBN: 978-1-953917-06-5
Ebook ISBN: 978-1-953917-05-8

First Printing, 2021

Edited by Elizabeth Lance
Book Cover Design by Nisha Franco
Published by Serpentine Creative LLC www.serpentinecreative.com

UNFORGETTABLE VALENTINE

STELLA WILLIAMS

Serpentine Creative LLC

Contents

I

Sinai pulled her wool coat tight around her body. Whoever decided that showing up to your man's place half-naked in a trench coat had obviously never done so in the winter, but it wasn't their fault. It was hers. She'd decided to surprise Carter as an early Valentine's Day present. Especially considering he'd been roped into a business trip and would be on a plane for the holiday.

She'd decided a spontaneous nightcap was the perfect send-off before they were separated for a week on the most romantic day of the year. An icy gust of wind forced her to tuck her head. It was so strong she nearly slid across the icy pavement. Another miscalculation on her part, not wearing proper shoes and just switching into heels once she was safely at his doorstep.

Impulsive wasn't a word anyone would describe Sinai as. Her entire life was run by a meticulously ordered schedule. A schedule she rarely deviated from without good reason. A fact that had caused many an argument with Carter in the past. Still, he understood her now, which made this all the more a surprise. She'd told him she couldn't meet him for dinner because she had to work late.

He hadn't even complained about it, although she could

see the disappointment in his face. So here she was, trying to make it up to him, braving the cold wind and icy streets. Another icy gust blew. This time she was on an incredibly sketchy piece of ice, and her coat caught the wind like a sail.

"Ahhh!" She screamed as she flew backward, losing her balance. She let go of her coat to try and catch herself in the fall, but instead of hard concrete, her back and hands met warm soft flesh. "Oh my God, I am so sorry." She jumped to her feet and turned to help whoever she'd landed on.

Embarrassed, she reached out her hand just as the man looked up at her. His eyes went wide, and his mouth fell open. For a moment, Sinai was confused until another blast of cold air made her realize she was completely exposed. Not only had she landed on top of someone, but her coat had blown wide open, revealing the red lace teddy she wore underneath.

Appalled, she turned away and snatched her coat closed. "Sorry," she muttered before taking off down the street.

* * *

Dominic Westmoore lay dumbfounded on the icy ground. He'd kept his distance from the woman walking ahead of him because he hadn't wanted to seem like a creeper. Yet, he'd felt compelled to follow her when he'd seen she was walking the dark streets alone at night. No one in their right mind would be out on the streets on a night like tonight. With Valentine's Day being tomorrow, most people were undoubtedly taking the chilly temperatures as an excuse to express their love in private. This late at night, even restaurants were closed.

Dominic himself wouldn't be out this late if he hadn't lost his never-ending battle with his mother and setting him up on blind dates. He'd been rude and left his mother alone with the Freemans at the restaurant, slipping away after paying the bill. Under different circumstances, he may have stayed and put up with being the trick pony for his mother's sake but not for Mina Freeman.

His mother would kill him when she found out, but Dominic had to draw the line somewhere, and Mina Freeman was definitely a line he didn't dare cross again. Usually, his mother wasn't pushy about his dating prospects. If it weren't for his cousin Bechet dating Isis Hale, there wouldn't be an issue. Now Dom's mother had lost her mind talking about weddings and grandchildren with his Aunt Melinda. It was one thing if the meeting had been with an actual business partner. It was crazy that his mother had even tried to pass the dinner off as strictly business in the first place.

It took all of half a second for Dom to realize the dinner was more than just business. Sure, Mr. Freeman had been a long-time business partner of his mother's. Still, Mina had nothing to do with it and had no reason to be there other than as an excuse to get close to him. His mother should have known better. Maybe three years ago, he would have been okay with the arrangement, but certainly not now.

He'd been pissed and decided a quick walk around the block would cool him off quickly, and then he could head home. Instead, here he was, with dirty street ice melting into his slacks and staring after the sexy damsel in distress who was currently sprinting away from him. The image of her in that lacy get-up was one he wasn't bound to forget soon.

He got up slowly, his hip a little worse for wear after the

fall. His arm, however, was tangled in the thin leather strap of the woman's purse.

"Dammit!"

He looked back down the street. The woman was still in view. He decided to try and catch up with her if he could. Being out in this cold in that get-up was one thing. Being out in the cold dressed like that without money and a phone, well, that was asking for trouble. He had no choice. He took off after the woman, he called out to her, but his voice was swallowed by the howling wind.

At least, her destination hadn't been too far. The lobby to the apartment building was closed at this hour, but luckily the door hadn't fully closed behind her, and Dom could go right in. He caught her just outside the elevators.

"Excuse me!"

The woman ignored him, so he tapped her on the shoulder. She turned to look at him, fire in her deep brown eyes before she recognized him. Her eyes bugged, and he couldn't help but smile.

"You dropped your purse."

He offered the brown leather bag to her, and the tense set of her shoulders relaxed. She even gave him a brief smile.

"Thank you for returning it."

Her voice was soft and sweet. Like vocal cotton candy. Nothing like how he expected based on her appearance. Her hair was slicked back into a severe ponytail. Her red wool coat and red lace undergarments did not reflect the soft innocence she exuded when speaking. She was giving him full naughty teacher vibes. It was definitely a turn-on for him. Dom had half a mind to ask her for her number, but she was obviously already spoken for. It was the night before Valentine's, after all. Whoever she'd dressed up for was a lucky man indeed.

"No problem."

He watched as she checked her belongings. She was smart too. Not saying he wasn't trustworthy, but she didn't know him from Adam. She looked up at him and raised an eyebrow.

"Are you expecting some sort of reward?"

He scrunched up his face before he realized he had, in fact, lingered longer than was necessary.

"Uh, no. Sorry. I just... Have a good night." He turned to leave just as the elevator dinged.

He couldn't help glancing over his shoulder to make sure she got into the elevator safely, but instead, she was standing stalk. Still, her hands clenched into fists so tight he was afraid her perfectly manicured nails would draw blood. He followed her gaze to the elevator, where a slim man and a busty blonde were making out. Each of them had matching suitcases at their side. They were so caught up in each other they didn't even notice when the door slid closed again.

* * *

"Are you fucking kidding me!"

Sinai marched over to the elevator to press the button and open the doors on her cheating now ex-boyfriend, but before she got there, a male hand grabbed her arm.

"You don't want to do that."

She whirled around on the presumptuous stranger, and when she saw it was the man she ran into before she snapped. She just started punching at his massive chest and cursing at him as if he was the one that she'd just caught cheating on her.

To his credit, the man just let her. It wasn't until she was exhausted that she noticed he had slowly backed her into a corner, shielding her from her ex and anyone passing by as she lost her shit.

She fell against his chest, tears streaming down her face.

"Shhh, it's okay."

He stroked her back, not in a sexual way but in a comforting way, and that just made her feel worse. This total stranger was so incredibly nice to her.

She pushed out of his grasp and wiped away her tears as best she could.

"No, it's not, but thank you."

With that, she spun on her heels and stormed out of her ex's apartment building.

She was just in time to see her ex pulling off in the cab to the airport with his secretary and apparently mistress. She pulled out her phone and called for a cab herself. There was no way she was walking back home right now; the wind had gotten worse, and snow had begun to fall. It looked as if an unforeseen blizzard was about to hit.

Sinai pulled her coat tighter around her, tucking her hands into the warm folds.

"You should wait inside."

Sinai looked behind her. It was that man again.

She looked toward the apartment lobby. She knew it was cozy inside, but all she could think about was seeing Carter and his secretary. At least for once, this evening, luck was on her side. A cab turned the corner just as she was about to go back inside.

She slid into the cab and was surprised when the guy slid in next to her.

"Do you mind if we share? I'll pay. It'll be hell getting another ride in a storm like this."

"That's for sure. This is my last fare of the night," the driver confirmed.

Sinai wanted to say no. She'd already been overexposed to this stranger in more ways than one. Yet, after all he'd done for her in the last hour, sharing a cab was the least she could do.

"Uh, sure, but have him drop you off first."

"Are you sure? I mean, you obviously walked here, your place is bound to be closer, and it seems unfair to make the driver go so far out of his way on a night like this."

"I'm sure," she said without hesitation.

"Where too?" the cabbie asked.

The man rattled off his address, and Sinai almost felt like changing her mind. His place was on the other side of town in the warehouse district. It was mostly industrial businesses and factories but was slowly being gentrified and turned into upscale condos and lofts. The cabbie obviously wanted to get this fare over with because he shot off before she could say she'd changed her mind.

Besides, he was already driving in the opposite direction of where she lived. She sighed and silently prayed the storm didn't get too bad for the return trip to her neighborhood. Sinai stared out of the window. She didn't even know this man's name, and she was too embarrassed to share any more about herself right then. She watched the snowfall become heavier, and the wind whipped up giant plumes of freshly fallen snow. The cab driver was forced to slow his speed to a crawl. The lack of visibility and the wind blew the small SUV here and there across the icy streets.

By the time they reached the man's neighborhood, the cabbie was cursing the heavens and hunched over the steering wheel to get a better view. A posture that was in vain because the snow's thickness limited visibility to just a few feet in front of the car. If it weren't for the GPS, she was sure the cabbie wouldn't have been able to find the place they were headed.

The cab driver's radio squawked about emergency procedures as he finally inched to the curb.

"I'm sorry, Miss, but I've got to call it. My company doesn't want us out right now. It's a liability."

Sinai's eyes bugged.

"Where the hell am I supposed to go?" she snapped.

"Did your date go well? Maybe your boyfriend will give you shelter for the night."

"He's not my...." Sinai didn't finish the sentence as the man beside her opened the cab door, and a gust of chilly air froze the words in her throat.

"No problem, Sir. Have a good night."

The man grabbed her arm and pulled her from the car. Sinai was too stunned and too cold to fight as he ushered her into what looked like an abandoned warehouse. Only one light bulb shown above the doorway. The man keyed in an entry code, and the metal door clicked as it unlocked.

"I know this isn't ideal, but I have plenty of space. You won't be bothered by me."

Sinai was glad to escape the cold and ice. The cab had already gone, and she was stuck. She pulled her phone out and dropped a geotag and a quick message to her sister that she was forced to take shelter with a strange man for the night.

It didn't surprise her that her phone began to ring immediately. It was a video call from her sister.

"Girl! What is your problem? How did you get yourself in this mess? Where is Carlos?"

Sinai rolled her eyes. Amayah had never gotten Carter's name right, and after three years of dating, Sinai was sure it was on purpose.

"Unexpected and unforeseen circumstances. How could I have known sharing a cab would end up with me having to stay with the man."

"Do you at least know his name? Send me a picture of his face and his place! Do you still have the mace I gave you for Christmas?"

The man snorted a laugh.

Sinai looked up at him, confused until she realized her phone was on speaker and not coming through her headset. She flushed with embarrassment. At least this time, it wasn't because she was inadvertently showing him her goodies. Sinai tightened her coat around herself just to be sure.

"Nai! Are you listening?" Amayah's voice felt like it was coming through a bullhorn instead of her phone's small speaker. Sinai shouldn't have answered the call.

It wasn't like he was just over her shoulder either. He was standing only a few feet away. His coat was discarded on a large rack made of industrial meat hooks. Noticing her discomfort, the man crossed the room and took the phone from Sinai's hands. He disconnected her headset before speaking.

"Hello, my name is Dominic Westmoore. I assure you; your sister is safe with me for the night. I promise to send her safely home when the storm lets up. Let me give you a tour and show you where she will be staying."

Sinai didn't have to assume how he figured out she and Amayah were sisters. They were identical twins. One of the main reasons they both had moved away from their small hometown just outside of Langsmith, California. Only Amayah had been smart and moved for work instead of fake love as Sinai had. Amayah had warned her about moving just because of a relationship. She should have heeded her sister's warning. Despite the many other great aspects of Mulberry, the main reason she'd made the move had turned out to be a complete bust. She should have known when Carter insisted on Sinai having her own place instead of moving in with him.

The wind howled outside, and Sinai glanced at the small pane of glass above the front door. It was too dark to see much more, but the snow accumulating on the edges of the window gave her the inkling that this wasn't going to be a small storm.

When she turned back to Dominic, he was already moving away from the door. She followed as he gave Amayah a virtual tour of his place. They had been standing in the entryway, a bland space of grey concrete and dull industrial furnishing. To the right was another heavy door, which he said led to his studio. He didn't elaborate on what the studio was for, but he didn't seem the artsy type, and Sinai didn't dare ask. It was enough she was stuck in his space until the morning.

Further down the hall, it opened up to a larger room. The red brick walls and oversized brown furniture looked manly and cozy, far from the industrial entrance. The kitchen was little more than a kitchenette along one wall, but the focal point was the massive metal furnace in the room's middle. It seemed almost out of place if she didn't already know this was an old warehouse.

She paused at the entrance to a dark hallway. Dom smirked at her before walking right in. Lights flickered on almost immediately.

"As you can see, most of the lighting in the public area is motion sensor activated. My room is at the end of the hall."

He positioned the phone, so Sinai's sister could see down the hall to the door at the very end, "and here," he turned slowly to the left and opened the door there, "Is where your sister will stay."

Sinai peeked around his shoulder to take a look at the room. It was small but well-appointed. A queen-sized bed with grey linens neatly stacked at the foot. A small chest of drawers on the opposite wall and the door next to that appeared to be the private bathroom entrance.

The walls were the same red brick as in the front room—nothing fancy and, she noted, no obvious place for a camera to be hidden. Dom turned around, and Sinai was too late to take a step back. He bumped into her sending her falling back.

"Crap!"

He fumbled her phone with one hand as he reached to catch her with the other. His hand clasped onto her coat, but the momentum of her fall was too much. Instead of steadying her, he pulled her coat from her body, exposing her once again.

Sinai hit the ground with a thud. Her exposed buttocks slapping the cold concrete flooring. "Ouch!"

"Sorry, I didn't see you behind me." Dom grimaced and dropped her coat on top of her.

Sinai snatched her coat to her chin and sighed. "It's not your fault. I shouldn't have been so close."

He reached out a hand to help her up, but she ignored it. Contact with Dominic Westmoore somehow always ended up with her on her ass, either physically or emotionally. She didn't want to take any further risk. Once standing, she held out her hand for her phone.

He handed her phone to her, and Sinai put on a smile for her sister's sake.

"Amayah, I'm going to be fine. I'll call you in the morning." She hung up the call before Amayah could protest or ask any more questions.

"Would you like some tea before calling it a night? Maybe a shirt to sleep in? You must be freezing," Dominic offered.

A cup of tea did sound good, but she just wanted this night to be over, so Sinai shook her head and pulled her coat tighter around herself.

"Thank you, but no, goodnight, Mr. Westmoore."

She stepped around him and into the guest room before closing the door behind her. Now with something substantial between her and one of two men she hoped never to see again, Sinai let her emotions catch up to her. All the anger, all the sadness, the fear, and embarrassment flooded her consciousness and streamed down her face as hot tears.

Sinai moved over to the bed and spread out the linens before crawling under the thick gray comforter. She would allow herself to be in her feelings for just one night, one night in this strange room in a stranger's house, and tomorrow she would get back to her real life.

"That's right, Nai. This isn't your reality. It's a minor detour. tomorrow, we'll get back to where we need to be," she whispered to herself.

* * *

Dom stood in front of the guest bedroom door for longer than was necessary. Hell, even a second was longer than necessary after she basically fled from him. He pressed his palm to the cool metal of the door.

"Sleep well," he sighed.

A tiny ache settled into his stomach, and he headed back down the hall to the main living space. He made sure everything was locked up tight before heading back to his own room for the night. He was just crawling under the covers when his phone began to ring. He looked over at the screen and nearly cursed. If there was any person he wanted to hear from less this evening, it would be Mina Freeman. He hit the ignore button, not caring that she knew he was awake, and sent her to voicemail. Hopefully, she would get the hint. Things were over between them, had been for a long time. The more Dom thought about it, there hadn't really been them. Just Mina using him as a springboard into the Westmoore family.

His phone buzzed again. This time it was just a text. He ignored it, it was late, and he was tired. Besides, he'd much rather think of the beautiful Sinai who was resting just down the hall. If they had met under different circumstances, he might have entertained asking her out. Now though, he needed to keep his cool just to not look like a total creep.

Dom turned out the lamp on his nightstand and settled into sleep. Only his brain and body had other ideas. Every time he closed his eyes, all he could picture was the sight of Sinai standing in front of him. That lacy scrap of lingerie doing nothing to hide her petite curves and glowing mahogany skin. Even with the sexy get-up, there was a sweetness about her that made her all the more enticing. The innocent gasp she made when she realized how exposed she had been to him, the real pain and frustration she'd released on him after seeing her lover with someone else.

He realized that it wasn't a mere physical attraction that was keeping him awake. No, it was something more. He instinctually wanted to protect her. He wanted to get up and go to her and make sure that she was okay. To hold her in his arms and comfort her as she cried. Most of all, he wanted to pummel the man who had obviously broken her heart.

It was silly, really. He didn't even know her. She was a complete stranger, and yet he wanted to avenge her as if it were his own sister who had been hurt. Maybe that was it. Perhaps he was triggered by his own relationship failings and fears for his younger sister, that he was getting unnecessarily worked up over a complete stranger.

Yes, that was it. He was projecting, and he needed to stop it. It would do him no good to keep along his current trail of thought. He turned onto his side and pulled his comforter over his head. He could finally get some rest, and once the morning came, his head would be clearer, and Sinai would be gone.

2

The smell of burning wood and coffee brought Sinai out of her deep slumber. She blinked her eyes open slowly, her head pounding as if she'd been out all-night drinking. Her eyes stung, but she forced them open anyway. Wiping her hand down her face, she took in her surroundings. "Where the hell am I?" This was definitely not Carter's place. That was when the events of last night came flooding back. Her run-in with Dominic Westmoore and the super embarrassing fit she'd thrown after catching Carter with his secretary. She bit her lip and groaned, throwing herself back onto the bed and tossing the covers back over her body.

"Stupid, stupid, stupid, Nai!" she chastised herself.

Sinai sat up and grabbed for her phone, which was on the nightstand next to the bed. At least she had remembered to plug it in last night. It was fully charged, and luckily the storm last night hadn't messed with cell service. She checked the weather, and her heart sunk even further. The storm last night had been worse than she imagined. Powerlines had been knocked down, streets were covered in ice and snow. The worst part was that the storm wasn't entirely over, so the city had decided to wait until it was before clearing the streets for traffic. An emergency stay-at-home order was in effect.

"Fuck me," Sinai cursed.

She'd hoped to be able to make a quick and easy getaway, but not even a rideshare would be available now. She was stuck. Alone with a strange man in said peculiar man's house for at least another full day and night. Sinai sent a text to her sister.

S: *The storm is only supposed to get worse. I'm stuck here for another day.*

A: *Have you talked to Casey? He okay with you being stuck with another man?*

Sinai rolled her eyes.

S: *Casey can take a flying fucking leap for all I care.*

Sinai's phone began to ring almost immediately.

"Do I need to catch a flight?" Amayah said as soon as Sinai answered the phone.

"You couldn't get out here even if you wanted to, and no, you don't. I'm okay."

"No, you aren't. I should have known there was more to this story, so spill."

Sinai sighed heavily and leaned back against the wood headboard of the bed. She hated that she was getting choked up all over again. She'd cried so much last night; she shouldn't have any water left in her body to cry anymore.

"I went to surprise Carter before his supposed business trip, and I caught him with his secretary."

Sinai had to hold the phone away from her ear as Amayah let out a string of not-so-empty threats and curses toward Carter. She didn't put the phone back up to her ear until Amayah took a deep breath and said her name calmly.

"Sinai, I'm not going to say I told you so. I know you're

hurting right now. I'm sorry Carter turned out to be the ass-hole I always said he was."

"It's not your fault. You've always had good instincts when it came to men. I should have learned to listen to you after Chance."

Amayah snorted with laughter at the mention of Sinai's high school boyfriend.

"Oh yeah, let's just say you should probably avoid men with names that begin with C from now on."

"Right, anyway. I promise I'm fine, or I mean I will be. I'm more upset about being cheated on than losing Carter."

As Sinai said the words, she realized they were true. Even as she'd lashed out at her handsome stranger, her rage had been more about being led on than the end of her relationship with Carter. If Sinai was honest, they hadn't truly been a couple in love. They had been a couple of convenience, and she'd been too stubborn to see all the signs that things weren't meant to continue with Carter after his move. She should have never followed him to Mulberry. Should have never tied her hopes of the future on a man who hadn't even wanted to live with her after years of dating.

Sinai pulled the covers up to her chin.

"Okay, I understand but, Nai. Don't let him get to you. He wasn't man enough for you. You are beautiful, smart, and en-terprising. That man child didn't know what he had, and you deserve so much better. Just take this time to fall in love with yourself again, okay?"

"Ugh, I hate feeling so unwanted. Like I dressed up in lin-gerie and a trench coat for his ass."

Amayah snorted again. "Are you serious? You're holed up

with that hottie in nothing but some lingerie? Girl! I know I just said to take your time, but maybe you being stuck with Mr. Hottie is a good thing."

Sinai scowled. "I know you aren't suggesting what I think you are," she said.

"I sure as hell am. I mean, why waste good lingerie. I'm not saying sleep with the guy, but a little flirtatious banter could be fun. Maybe sneak a pic of you and him and social media dump Carver's trifling ass."

Sinai laughed this time. "You are out of your mind."

"Do or don't. Hell, he probably has a girlfriend who is pissed as fuck about being away from him on Valentine's Day. Anyway, just be safe and definitely be careful, okay. I gotta run."

Amayah hung up before Sinai could reply.

Sinai tossed her head back and stared at the ceiling. The fates really had a way of fucking with her when it came to relationships. She sat in bed until the smell of bacon wafted into the room, making her stomach grumble. She slid out of bed and, for a moment, considered snagging the sheet to wrap around her body, but then she changed her mind. He'd already seen her in her lingerie multiple times at this point. She followed the delicious smell from the bedroom and into the living space. Her stranger had his back turned to her as he scooped the crispy bacon from the pan in his hand and onto a paper towel.

He was wearing a white tank that lay perfectly between his shoulder blades, extenuating his broad shoulders and muscular arms. The ribbed tank drew her eyes down to his thick grey sweats that hugged the generous bubble of his high buttocks. She bit her lip and leaned against the wall to enjoy the view. Maybe Amayah was right. A little flirting just might be in order. If he didn't already have a girlfriend, that was. A man like Dom was probably the quintessential lady's man. His bachelor pad seemed laid out to maximize the potential of a hookup, from the large brown leather couches that could easily fit two bodies horizontal to the plush rug in front of the massive industrial hearth that was currently ablaze. She could just imagine the feel of it chafing her back as his enormous body moved fluidly above hers, the heat of the massive flames nothing compared to the heat that stirred in her loins.

Without a second thought, Sinai let her hand trail up her thighs to the apex of her legs. The thin lace thong she wore was crotchless, and her fingers were coated with her arousal as she naughtily touched herself. Dom was busy in the kitchen, the bacon done. He opened the small oven and retrieved a thick stack of pancakes. She didn't know what was making her mouth water more, the thought of those fluffy pancakes and crisp bacon or the man who was busily preparing the meal for her.

Her index finger brushed her clit, and she gasped at how sensitive she was. She had never been this sensitive before, not even after climax with Carter. Her gasp caught Dom's attention, and he looked up. His deep brown eyes meeting her gaze, a soft smile stretching his lips and revealing perfectly white teeth and the sexiest dimple Sinai had ever seen.

"Good morning," he said.

His deep baritone washed over her and her pussy clenched tight before pleasure exploded through her body. She flushed red as a beet as her body orgasmed. She bit back the moan threatening to escape the back of her throat. Still, she didn't dare stop stroking herself, didn't dare deny herself the rolling pleasure coursing through her body as he stared intently at her. Belatedly she realized he was waiting for her reply. Could he not see what she was doing? Was he just being polite at her wanton display?

She kept her gaze locked with his, not willing to risk moaning out loud and giving herself away, any more than she was willing to let the intense orgasm die with embarrassment. She deserved this. She needed this, and to be honest, she was far past embarrassment with Dom.

* * *

Dom cocked his head to the side as Sinai stood leaning against the entry to the hallway. He smirked. She was probably too shy to come closer. He noticed she wasn't wearing her coat as a shield this morning. Her body on full display, he trained his gaze on her face to keep from embarrassing himself. Normally he didn't mind if a female guest in his home caught a glimpse of what he was slinging but not Sinai. Not with how they had met and ended up in this situation.

She was flushed, a deep red beneath the smooth chocolate of her skin, tiny beads of perspiration cropped up around her brow. The neat ponytail she wore was now frizzing, and the flyways framed and stuck to her damp skin. His fingers itched to touch them. To smooth the strands back into place.

He watched as her flush grew deeper, she caught her full bottom lip between her teeth, and for a moment, Dom forgot he had even spoken.

"Good morning," he said before he realized he was repeating himself.

Sinai's eyes grew wide, and her mouth fell open, a sigh that sounded suspiciously like a moan escaped her lips. His dick jumped in his pants, and he quickly turned away.

"How do you like your eggs?"

What kind of question was that?

There was nothing overtly sexual about the moment. If anything, it was tense and awkward as hell, but somehow Dom was detecting the smell of sex in the air, the delicate musk of a wet pussy ready for the taking. He fumbled the carton of eggs in his hand and only out of sheer luck was able to avoid a mess on the kitchen floor, even as he was on the verge of making a mess of himself over Sinai.

Get your shit together, Dom.

He took a deep breath and turned back to Sinai. Fuck the eggs. From this vantage point, she was no longer shielded by the couch. He could see her from head to toe, and the last thing he suspected was to see her, legs wide and touching herself as she stared directly at him.

He tossed the eggs on the counter and made a move toward her, but she put her free hand up.

"Don't," she said.

Her voice the sexiest of pleas. He stopped in his tracks, afraid she may turn and run.

"Sinai," he began but was cut off as she moaned again.

Arching her back, she closed her eyes. He watched as her fingers dipped in and out of her pussy. He licked his lips as he watched her.

"Are you cumming?"

She smiled. "Only when you talk," she said.

Dom was unprepared for just how much of a turn on that was. His dick was so hard he could probably do push-ups with it at this point. "You like my voice?"

She moaned.

"Does your pussy like my voice?"

She cried out an enthusiastic, "Yes!"

It took every ounce of his restraint to keep himself in place, to not take another step toward her. To keep his hands firmly at his sides instead of touching her or touching himself.

"Keep touching yourself," he said and marched back over to the kitchen. He grabbed the plate of food he had been making for her and brought it over to where she was standing. Sinai didn't protest as he got close to her. So, close he could feel the heat radiating from her body but not touching her. He wouldn't dare touch her without her permission.

"I'm going to feed you, but I want you to keep pleasuring yourself while I do it."

Sinai met his gaze before nodding slowly.

"How many times can you cum?" he asked.

"I... I don't know."

Dom picked up a slice of bacon and fed it to her. Her pink tongue sliding over the piece of meat before she closed her mouth around it was enough to have him leaking. She chewed slowly, a deep hum of gratification reverberating from the back of her throat.

"Keep doing that, and I won't be able to give you space."

"Fuck, I'm cumming again," she cried.

Her hands pumped faster. He could hear the sloppy sucking as her release coated her fingers and palms. He waited until her movements slowed before offering her another bite.

"How many times have you cum?"

"How many times have you spoken to me?"

"My voice really does it for you, huh?"

"Yes," she gasped, "and also your ass in those sweatpants."

Dom laughed and turned to the side, popping his booty out like women did on social media.

"This ass?"

She nodded enthusiastically, her hands working faster over her flesh. He rewarded her with a bite of pancake.

"Well then, let's see how many I can give you before this plate of food is done."

"Ugh, I don't think my legs will hold me much longer."

Dom noted the slight tremble in her knees. He took the plate over to the coffee table and set it down before going back to Sinai. "I'm going to carry you to the couch. I want you to keep working yourself up for me, okay?"

He waited for Sinai to nod in approval before he swept her into his arms. He could feel her body shaking with yet another release. For a moment, he contemplated stopping her. Multiple orgasms were great, but he didn't want to overload her. She had already been through so much yesterday. It was one of the reasons he was restraining himself now. People dealt with grief and anger in different ways, and it seemed Sinai dealt with them in orgasms. Multiple intense orgasms that he wished he could do more to bring her but knew better than to try.

He was about to set her gently on the couch, but she clutched him tightly with her free arm.

"I want to sit in your lap," she said.

Dom raised an eyebrow at her.

"Be more specific."

"I want you to hold me and feed me while I make myself cum. I want you to talk to me but not touch me intimately. I need to make myself cum. I don't want you to do it because I need to be selfish and all about me right now."

Dom couldn't help but chuckle. "That might be a pretty tall order, sweetheart, but I understand. Am I allowed to touch myself while you get off?"

Sinai bit her lip and seemed to consider his question for a moment before shaking her head.

"No, I mean not right now, maybe later. I need to think about that more."

Dom's balls tightened at the idea of being perpetually hard while she came to her heart's content. It wasn't a bad thought; actually, he just wasn't sure how long he could hold out. He carefully settled onto the couch, cradling her in his lap and doing his best to avoid pressing his erection into her exposed ass cheeks.

She leaned against his chest. "It's okay if I feel you, just don't move too much," she said.

Dom relaxed; her head settled against his chest right over his heart. He had just enough reach to bring food to her mouth periodically as he began to talk about anything and everything he could think of. Her soft mewling and satisfied moans were music to his ears. The plate of food was long gone; she was still at it for hours. When she finally relaxed against him, sleep having overcome her, Dom realized he himself hadn't eaten. His own plate still on the counter in the kitchen, yet he didn't dare move so soon. Dom cradled Sinai in his arms, her soft, even breathing lulling him to sleep. He could eat later. For now, he was too busy enjoying the softness of this well-satisfied woman in his arms.

* * *

It was dark and cold when Sinai woke up, she quickly realized she wasn't in the guest bed, but on the leather couch, she shifted and found that Dom was gone. A tan throw blanket lay discarded on the floor. She grabbed the blanket and wrapped it around herself. She was exhausted and yet utterly satisfied. Her body ached from the marathon orgasms she'd given herself while cradled lovingly in Dom's arms.

Sinai had no idea what had overcome her, but she was glad she hadn't shied away when Dom caught her fucking herself against the wall. In fact, if given a nice warm bath and another hour or so, she could probably fuck herself some more. Sinai had never really been into self-gratification, but now she definitely saw the appeal.

"You're awake," Dom said, shuffling into the room from the hallway. He moved over to the fireplace and hefted several massive logs into the hearth, rekindling the embers into massive flames. In a minute, the room had warmed back up, and Sinai shrugged out of the throw blanket. Dom brought her a glass of water from the kitchen.

"Thank you," she said.

"After the day you just had, you need to stay hydrated."

Sinai laughed. "No, I mean, thank you for putting up with my I don't know what to call it earlier. I'm not like this usually."

Dom sat next to her, not close but not too far to where she felt he was withdrawing from her. "Everyone deals with their emotions differently, and I can't say I didn't enjoy watching the way you deal with yours."

A blush crept into her cheeks, and she reached for the throw again, suddenly feeling incredibly exposed and shy. Dom noticed and stood up.

"I probably should have offered you a change of clothes earlier."

Sinai stood and grabbed his hand.

"Dom?"

He turned to her, concern in his eyes.

"Do you have a tub?"

Dom laughed.

"Yes, in my room."

"Do you mind if I borrow it? I could really use a soak."

Dom nodded. "I'm sure you could. Come on. I'll show you how it works and gives you some privacy."

Sinai followed Dom into his bedroom. It was much larger than she expected. It was practically its own apartment minus a kitchen. In the middle of the room was a massive bed. Like custom-sized massive, fit a whole family massive. The sheets were tangled up at the foot of the bed, and she wondered if he'd had his own pleasure time after she'd fallen asleep.

"I sleep kind of wild. Having a big bed ensures I don't fall off," he said and quickly tossed the covers in place as best he could.

To the right of the room was a glass brick partition, and Dom led her there. He wasn't lying about having a tub but to be more accurate, he had a bath, like a European-style bath.

She could just imagine him naked and lounging like a king in his private oasis. Her clit tingled, and she silently cursed herself for asking about the tub. She wanted to relax, not work herself up again.

Dom showed her how to work the temperature controls on the bath before disappearing to bring her a set of towels and a thick blue robe that she knew would absolutely dwarf her and would definitely smell like Dom's cologne.

"Just holler if you need anything. Otherwise, come out when you're ready, and I'll make dinner."

Dinner? It's that late already?"

Dom nodded.

"Yeah, breakfast was more a brunch. We both slept in," he said.

Dom left her alone in the bath, and she stripped out of her lingerie. Tossing it to the side, she really wanted to toss it in the trash, but then she would have nothing to wear home. She would have to toss it later. There was no way it was staying in her collection, no matter how expensive it had been. She bought it specifically for Carter, and now it was just a reminder of how much a shit he was. That and how wanton she was with Dom.

She sank into the warm water, her body relaxing, and she massaged her arms and legs. It felt great, but it also felt lonely and quiet. Too quiet. Quiet enough for her to start thinking about Carter and all the time and energy she had wasted on him.

"Dom!"

His name was on her lips before she could stop herself. He was there in a matter of moments.

"Yes, Madame?" He bowed deeply at her, and she laughed.

"Come join me. I mean unless you have more important things to do. I mean, I know you do, but..."

She stopped talking as Dom stripped down to his boxers and waded in with her.

"You don't want to be alone. You need me to talk some more. I've just about run out of mundane stories."

Sinai pulled him to rest between her legs. Wrapping her arms around his neck, she pressed a soft kiss to his chin.

"Tell me about the first love interest who broke your heart."

* * *

When Sinai kissed him, the last thing he expected was for her to ask about his first heartbreak, yet it was totally on-brand for her actions that day.

He sat down and pulled her on top of him. Her naked body pressed against his bare skin made him glad he hadn't removed his boxers, otherwise talking would be the last thing that happened in the bath. She rested her head on his shoulder, and he was careful not to sink so deep into the water that her hair got wet.

"The first and hopefully last person to break my heart was Mina Freeman in the ninth grade. I had a huge crush on her, and I was foolish enough to tell her that I planned to make her my wife one day."

"Seriously? Ninth grade?"

"I'm a man who knows what he wants, alright?"

"And how did she turn you down. Obviously not gently."

Dom sighed. "The crazy part is she didn't. Not really. She

told me she would only marry me if I grew up to be rich and powerful like her daddy."

"So, it was you who ran from that entitled little snot?"

"Hell no! I let Mina string me along for years. She was never my girlfriend. Just made sure every other girl knew not to get serious about me."

Sinai sat up and looked into his eyes. He averted his gaze. Everyone in his circle knew that he and Mina had something going, but no one knew the details. Apparently, not even he knew the whole story until it was too late.

"So, you broke up recently?"

"It's been three years since she eloped with an oil baron she met on a pleasure cruise."

"A fucking what! You're lying to me."

"I wish I was; I was a fool. I thought I loved her. I did everything I could to meet each of her stupid goalposts to finally be with her, and her ass runs off and gets married on a trip I paid for."

Sinai's smile faltered. "Oh my God! That's terrible. I hope she's miserable."

"She's divorced. The marriage lasted all of a year."

"Serves her right. Wait, you sound pretty certain about her being miserable. Are you still?"

Sinai started to move away from him, but he wrapped an arm around her waist and pulled her back to rest on his chest.

"If I still cared about her, I wouldn't be doing whatever this is with you. I'm loyal to a fault, but I'm not that stupid. She never wanted me. She just wanted what I thought I could give her until she got a better offer."

"You don't sound like you are over her," Sinai said.

Dom sighed and ran a hand over his face. "Maybe I'm not over her yet, but I'm damn sure done with her."

There was silence between them for a moment before Sinai began to kiss along his collarbone.

"How was your sex life with her," she asked.

Dom tensed. "I don't want to talk about that."

"That bad, huh." She laughed.

Dom sat up straighter and cupped her chin, bringing her in direct eye contact with him. "I've never had any complaints about my skills in bed."

"Women rarely complain directly to the men they sleep with."

"Mina isn't that type of woman. Besides, if anything, she was on the receiving end of a lot of pleasure by my hands."

"But not true the other way around?"

"Why are you so curious?"

Sinai shrugged and moved to the opposite side of the tub from him. "Misery loves company, I guess. Carter never told me outright that he had issues with our sex life, but there were hints. I thought I'd done enough when he stopped dropping them, but obviously, he'd just moved on to someone else."

Dom relaxed a little. At least the attention was off of his failed romantic life for now.

"This Carter boy is obviously the one lacking in this situation. You cum with such ease and such joy. Only a fool wouldn't want that."

Sinai laughed. "I'm actually the opposite. It would take hours of foreplay for such measly rewards. I would schedule our encounters just to ensure there was enough time for me to get mine."

Dom couldn't believe what he was hearing. No way in hell the orgasm-every-second-woman in front of him took hours to get warmed up.

"Exactly my point. Carter was not the guy for you. It took him hours to get you off when I literally read you the weather report, and you came apart twice."

Sinai smiled and then shrugged. "These aren't normal circumstances, and to be fair, I got myself off."

Dom wasn't going to let her off the hook. He surged across the tub and hovered over her, bending down, he whispered into her ear, "Cumulonimbus."

Sinai shuddered and moaned.

"Low-pressure formation."

Her eyes fluttered closed, and she bit her lip.

"Ninety percent chance of precipitation."

She arched her back and cried out. Dom swallowed her cry with his mouth, her tongue shot out to seek his, and that was what broke him. He lifted her from the tub and carried her wet naked body to his bed.

"I want you to fuck yourself. I want you to ride your hand like you would ride a dick. I want you to fondle your breasts, bite yourself, smack that ass. Whatever it takes, whatever turns you on."

Sinai lay breathless before him, fire dancing in her eyes. "And what about you?"

Dom smirked. "I'm just the scorekeeper. A spectator, if you will."

"Okay?"

"More than okay. Where is your phone?"

"I think it's still in the guest room. Why?"

"I'm going to record you so you can see just how fucking hot and beautiful you are. I'm going to use your phone, so you have full control over the footage."

* * *

Dom was gone before Sinai could reply. For a moment, she'd thought he was going to fuck her. She'd wanted him to fuck her, but part of her was glad he was abiding by her previous rules. They were still strangers, hell he might even be out of condoms, and that was why he was so eager to watch her pleasure herself. Maybe it was his own choice to remain unattached. Maybe he thought by sleeping with her, she would latch on to him like that crazy ass Mina chick he talked about.

She felt subconscious sitting wet and naked on his massive bed. She pulled her knees to her chest and wrapped her arms around herself. If she was completely honest, she was already worried about the repercussions of her actions. Would she regret this all once the storm cleared up and she could go back to reality? Would she have an awkward run-in with Dom in a few weeks and have to pretend she was a different person entirely.

The tingling of arousal she felt earlier was quickly turning into anxiety. She jumped when Dom came back into the room, her phone in his hand. He took one look at her, and the excited smile he wore faltered.

"Are you okay?" He came to her side and pulled her into his arms.

"Not really," she admitted. Tears began to stream down her face.

Dom wiped the first few away with his hand before he sighed and stood again.

"I'm sorry," she said.

Dom crossed the room to the set of drawers and pulled out a t-shirt.

"No need to be sorry."

She reached for the shirt, but he held it away, rolling it up before placing it over her head. Dom helped Sinai put his shirt on and then went to grab the clothes he'd discarded by the bath.

"Take all the time you need. I'm going to make us some food."

Sinai didn't know if she was glad that he seemed so understanding of her need for space or if she was dejected by the fact that yet another man was discarding her sexually.

She cuddled up to his pillow and allowed the tears to flow. Her heart ached something fierce, and yet she wasn't entirely sure it had anything to do with Carter. Sliding off the bed, Sinai grabbed her phone and left the room. Watching Dom cook was a much better distraction than lying alone in his bed, surrounded by his scent and her budding feelings of regret.

Dom smiled when he saw her, and she deposited herself on the couch. She picked up her phone to check social media. Maybe seeing what her friends were up to would help her not think about things for a while. All of her college friends were posting their Valentine's Day pictures with their boos or their self-celebrations for the single ones. She wished she was half as content as they looked on the *gram*.

At least she had never done the whole social media official thing with Carter. No need to have the embarrassment of changing your status from in a relationship to single, or it's complicated or whatever. She was just about to log off when there was a notification for a post-Carter tagged her in. She clicked the post and shook her head. That asshole had posted a picture of them together last Valentine's Day with a caption that stated, "Wishing I could be with my boo today."

Her blood pressure spiked, and she nearly chucked her phone across the room. *How dare he!*

She almost wrote a scathing comment on the post, but after three tries to convey the perfect amount of 'go fuck yourself,' she decided against it. She glanced over at Dom. He was shirtless, and she could tell he was definitely not wearing boxers under his sweatpants this time. A naughty idea crossed her mind. She pulled the hair tie from her hair and styled her hair into a sexy, just out-of-bed look before propping herself on the edge of Dom's couch.

Opening her front camera, she made sure to get a good shot of Dom in the background. He was looking down, so his face wasn't visible. She didn't want to make things complicated for him, but she wanted him to be in the shot. Sinai wearing his shirt and looking sexily tousled, while Dom cooked shirtless in the background; it was scandalous and precisely what she wanted.

Sinai took the shot quickly and typed out a quick caption. *Music note emoji; He keeps me warm #vday #mulberryblizzard*

She posted it before she could second-guess herself.

"Come to the island, foods ready."

Sinai nearly fell off her perch on the couch when Dom spoke. She caught herself just in time and moved to the barstool at the island. Dom had cooked a simple meal of broccoli, brown rice, and chicken breast, but it smelled heavenly.

"Thank you for taking care of me," she said, reaching out to squeeze Dom's hand.

He brought her hand to his lips and kissed her knuckles. "My pleasure, Madame."

Sinai scrunched up her face.

"Are you going to keep calling me Madame like I'm your grandmother?"

Dom snorted. "You sure as hell aren't my grandmother, and yes, I think it fits the way you dominate the shit out of me."

"Don't go making excuses for your submissive ass traits. I am nobody's Madame."

"I am not submissive," he said.

Sinai took a bite of her chicken and moaned as the rich flavor of rosemary and butter exploded in her mouth. Dom smirked at her show of enjoyment.

"You said you became rich and powerful for this Mina chick? What do you do for a living?"

Dom paused with his fork halfway to his mouth. "I should clarify that I am well off, not rich, and my influence comes more from my family than from anything I've done myself."

"So, you're a reluctant trust fund baby?" She slapped a hand over her mouth as soon as she realized she'd actually said that out loud.

Dom laughed and shook his head. "I guess you could say that. How long have you been in Mulberry?"

"How did you know I wasn't from here?"

"Anyone who is from Mulberry knows who my family is."

"That serious, huh?"

Dom nodded.

"So, tell me. Who is the great Dominic Westmoore?"

"Nah, I think I'll let you figure it out on your own," he said, a twinkle of mischief in his eyes.

"Whatever, it's fine. I checked the weather. The storm had blown over quicker than they thought. Clean up should reach here by tomorrow afternoon."

Sinai stuffed her mouth with food after dropping that bit of fact. Dom just nodded, and they continued eating in silence until both of their plates were clear. Dom picked up their plates and carried them to the sink. Sinai followed and elbowed him out of the way.

"You cooked. The least I could do is the dishes."

"You're a guest in my house. Go relax on the couch. I got this."

"Dom," she started to protest, but he pinned her against the counter and leaned in close to her.

"Go sit your hot ass on the couch before I show you just how dominant I can be right here on the kitchen counter," he growled.

Sinai smirked and bit her lip. "Was that supposed to be a threat?"

Sinai braced herself on the counter before pushing herself up. She spread her legs wide as soon as her butt hit the polished concrete.

Dom shook his head and laughed. "I thought you didn't want me to touch you?"

"I thought you were going to dominate me?"

Dom leaned in and kissed her. His lips were soft and teasing against hers. His hands slid up her thighs to cup her ass. Sinai leaned into him with a delicate sigh.

"The problem is I don't want to dominate your body. I want to dominate your heart and soul."

Sinai didn't know what to think about that. Lucky for her, Dom slid one thick digit across her pussy lips, and all thought ceased.

* * *

Dom had no idea why he'd just said that, and to make matters worse, he realized he actually meant it. He didn't know Sinai, but he wanted to get to know her. He wanted to make her smile, make her feel beautiful inside and out. He wanted to make her orgasm with his hands, his mouth, and his dick. Every red flag in the book was there.

She melted in his arms, whimpering softly as he coated his fingers with her arousal. Hell, he was going to wring every ounce of pleasure from her body he could before the inevitable. Sinai had said it herself the storm was clearing; he would have no reason to keep her here and knew that there was no way either of them should pursue this inappropriate attraction beyond the moment.

He pressed his fingers firmly to her clit as her hips rocked back and forth in slow, languid movements.

"That's it, Madame, I want you to use me. Ride my fingers like you rode your own."

She gripped his wrist and pulled his hand lower until his fingers teased her entrance.

"I'll let you call me Madame all you want if you slide those fingers inside," she said.

Dom buried his face in his neck and pressed his fingers in her pussy. Sinai was so wet her arousal pooled in the palm of his hand. He crooked his finger, rubbing along her inner walls until he found the g-spot. He tickled the sensitive area while pressing the palm of his hand against her clit. Sinai cried out, her body violently shaking with release.

"Dom!"

It was that moment Dom knew he was a goner. He may only have Sinai for this one night, but she would forever be a cherished memory in his heart.

3

Dom's heavy arm and leg were draped over Sinai's naked body when she woke up. She shook her head as she noticed all the sheets had been kicked to the ground overnight. Dom had not lied about being a wild sleeper. Thankfully she'd been too exhausted from their play to really mind. She carefully slid out of his grasp. Last night had been, well, the last day with Dom had been something else. Any thoughts of regret she may have had before were nowhere to be found. She would cherish this time with him probably for the rest of her life, but she didn't dare stick around for the awkward goodbye.

She found her lingerie still folded neatly by the bath and slipped it on. She had no other clothes to wear and didn't want to take his shirt home with her. It was best to make a clean break. Last night had been too emotional, and she didn't want to add to her already large case of relationship baggage. Dom was still resting as she snuck out of his room.

Her coat and purse were in the guestroom but her phone. She had no idea where it had ended up last night. After finger fucking her on the kitchen counter, they had followed through with Dom's idea of recording her making herself orgasm. That had been on the couch. After they had watched the replay in front of the hearth while he massaged her body.

It wasn't on the plush rug nor on the couch. She finally found it when her foot stepped on it, cracking the screen. It had been pushed half under the couch.

"Just my luck," she hissed as she examined the damage. Her phone was basically unusable now as the cracks spiderwebbed all the way across the screen.

There would be no easy escape now. She would need to use Dom's phone to call for a ride. Biting her lip, she headed back into his bedroom. Dom sat on his bed looking at his own phone with a deep scowl.

"Good morning." Sinai tried for light and unaffected by the sight of his massive body completely naked before her.

Dom looked up, his gaze not softening one bit. He turned his phone toward her.

"You posted this without my permission."

Sinai recognized the post in question almost immediately. The only problem was it wasn't on her account but on the front page of Mulberry Gazette Online.

Dominic Westmoore's New Blizzard Bae

"What the fuck!"

"Exactly my sentiments," Dom said.

"I'm so sorry." Sinai really was sorry. How in the world had they recognized him from just his abs? Was he really that well known? More importantly, how had they found her account to begin with?

"It's done now. I just wish there was more I could do about damage control."

"Can you just deny it's you in the photo? I mean, your face isn't seen."

Dom shook his head. "I was featured in the Gazette just

last month for the renovation to this warehouse. The photo spread included a picture of me cooking in my kitchen almost exactly like this only with clothes on."

"Fuck! I'll delete the post." Sinai raised her phone only to remember it was broken.

"It's too late for that. It's already made the papers. You happened to use the hashtag they started to get pictures of Valentine's Day couples during the blizzard. The most we can do is hope they focus on the blizzard clean-up tomorrow."

"I know you mentioned you were well-known, but I had no idea; I mean, I posted this before we even talked about that. It was stupid, and I'm sorry."

"Stop apologizing, Sinai. What's done is done."

He was angry with her, and he had every right to be. He'd abided by all of her rules and boundaries the last couple of days, and how had she repaid him? By taking a scandalous photo of him and posting it online. Tears began to well in her eyes. "I should go."

She turned and practically sprinted from the room. It didn't matter that her phone was broken, and she would have to walk miles in the cold to even have a chance of getting a ride back home. She just knew she needed to get out of there. Sinai made it to the front door. Flinging it open, she nearly ran into an elderly woman in an expensive fur coat.

She stumbled back right into Dom's arms. The older woman gasped and covered her eyes. "Dominic Tyrelus West-moore!"

The cold air hit Sinai's exposed skin, and she cursed before snatching her coat back closed. She tried to push away from

Dom, but he held her firmly in front of him. He was completely naked behind her.

"Give us a second, Mom, and I'll introduce you properly to my girlfriend."

Sinai spun around wide-eyed. Dom shot her a pleading look before dragging her back into his room, using her for cover.

"Girlfriend!" Sinai hissed as soon as they were in his room with the door closed.

Dom didn't answer her immediately. He went over to his drawers and pulled out a new shirt and sweats. He also tossed her a shirt and a pair of basketball shorts.

"Change into these. We'll talk after my mother leaves."

"Oh, hell no! We are talking about this now!"

Dom crossed the room and pulled her into his arms. He pressed a soft kiss to her lips, and the anger she felt before quickly melted into arousal. She softened against him and moaned.

"Please, Sinai."

He nipped at her lower lip, and all she could do was nod. Apparently, her body wasn't ready to get back to reality just yet. He pulled away, and they both got dressed. He took her hand before they headed into the living room where Dom's mother sat on the couch looking at her phone.

* * *

Sinai's grip on Dom's hand was like a vice. She was obviously not okay with this situation, but it was a little late for her to back out. At least Dom hoped she continued to play along. He was pissed about the picture thing, sure, but if he was honest, he was more upset that she had obviously intended to leave without saying goodbye. Now was most certainly not the time for him to make any sort of romantic move on Sinai, but he at least had hoped they could exchange numbers with the promise of maybe. In the future, of course, when she was over her asshole ex, and he wasn't dealing with Mina. Then she'd run into his mother, and yeah. There was no way he would be able to handle his mother without an explanation to her liking for what she had just seen.

"Mother," he said.

His mother looked up from her phone, the slight frown on her turning into a quick smile. It wasn't a real one. Dom knew his mother well enough to tell her real smile from her polite one.

"Son of mine. I had no idea you were seeing anyone. Especially not anyone seriously," she cut right to the chase.

Sinai tugged at his hand a little, but he couldn't let her show any signs of weakness here. His mother was a shark in the water, and not a drop of blood could be sensed, or they both would face her wrath. Well, mostly him.

"I was waiting until the holiday to make things official."

He was purposely vague. No extra information to get him or Sinai tripped up later. His mother laughed lightly, but a lead weight settled in his stomach.

"Official? Is that what they call monogamy these days?"

Dom felt Sinai tense by his side. This was going downhill fast.

"Like I said, this wasn't how I wanted to introduce you," Dom said.

"You still haven't introduced us," his mother said.

Dom sighed heavily and pulled Sinai closer to him.

"Mom, meet my girlfriend Sinai, Sinai, meet my mother, Regina Westmoore."

To her credit, Sinai's smile was genuine as she extended her hand to his mother, and even as his mother accepted her handshake like it was sopping wet with fish juice, the fact she hadn't ignored it completely was a sign she wasn't completely against the idea of Sinai as his girlfriend.

"It's a pleasure to meet you, Ms. Westmoore, even if under less-than-ideal circumstances."

"Likewise, Ms...." Dom's mother looked to him to fill in the gap, but Sinai was quick to jump in.

"Carlisle, Sinai Carlisle."

His mother looked between the two of them again. Dom didn't relax until his mother's own posture relaxed and she stood.

"Well, I would hate to intrude on your time together. Please, Dom, bring Ms. Carlisle to dinner this Sunday so she can be properly introduced to the family."

"I'll have to make sure Sinai is free, but yes, Mother, I will do my best to properly introduce her to the rest of the family soon."

* * *

Sinai bit the inside of her cheek to keep from cursing Dom out in front of his mother. What the hell was he thinking? What the hell was she thinking?

There was no reason she should have stayed. No reason for her not to have charged right out the door and let Dom clean up his own mess. Except it wasn't just his mess. It was hers for posting that damn photo, for letting Carter get to her over social media of all things and acting outside of her better judgment.

She forced a smile and stared what she hoped looked lovingly up at Dom even as she wanted to jam her heel right down on his bare toes.

"Of course, I have time on Sunday to meet your family," she turned to Mrs. Westmoore, "thank you for the invitation."

Mrs. Westmore smiled brightly and nodded. "That settles it. I shall see you both Sunday."

With that, Mrs. Westmoore strode out of the living room. Sinai didn't dare move from Dom's side until she heard the heavy thud of the metal front door closing solidly behind his mother. Then she pulled out of his grasp and marched toward the room to change.

"Sinai!"

"No! Nope! This is not okay!"

She began to strip out of his clothing, not caring that she was completely naked underneath. He'd seen it all at this point anyway, and she was too angry to be bothered with any false modesty.

"This isn't how I wanted this morning to go. Please let's talk this out and be reasonable."

Sinai grabbed her coat and wrapped it tightly around her body. She snagged the black silk tie she'd used on him the night before and used it to secure her coat firmly in place. There would be no further accidental exposures. As far as the lingerie, he could keep it as a memory or toss it. She never wanted to see it again.

"I feel like I am the only one being reasonable here. We're

strangers, Dom. I know I didn't act like it the last two days, and I really am sorry about the whole photo thing, but I can't do this."

She grabbed her purse and rushed out before he could stop her. He called her name again, but she didn't stop. She didn't dare look back either. She was just stepping out onto the side-walk when she realized she didn't have any shoes on. The ice bit into her skin before she yelped and jumped back, right into Dom's arms, again.

She growled and pouted in defeat.

"You have the two minutes it will take me to get my shoes to try and convince me to go along with this," she muttered.

Dom smirked before kissing her. "I'm going to need a bit more time than that."

4

Dom reached over to crank the heat up in his car. A smug smile on his face as Sinai relaxed into the heated leather seat and placed her hand on his thigh. He'd been able to convince her to spend another night with him, but they'd both had work to get back to, and Dom knew that he couldn't keep her locked up at his place forever. For a moment yesterday, he thought she was actually going to try and disappear on him. Every sane and rational part of him knew it was for the best that he let her go. She was dealing with heartbreak. He didn't want to be anyone's second choice or rebound guy, and yet here he was driving her home. He'd insisted after finding out her phone was busted, and she refused to wear his clothes home. No way would he allow her to take a cab or rideshare naked when he had a perfectly good car and a perfectly good reason to drive back into the city.

"Don't get any ideas. I'm just practicing for when we're in front of your family."

Dom took one hand off the steering wheel to take her hand in his.

"In front of my family, I'd prefer if we held hands like this. If you grab my thigh like that, dinner will be very short indeed."

Sinai laughed. It was light and airy, like butterflies hovering about. He loved the sound of it and wished to hear it more. He wanted to make her laugh more, make her smile. It was an instinct, a driving force within him right alongside the driving need to get in her pants.

He wasn't complaining about their time together, but there was only so much teasing a man could take. He'd only allowed himself one release her entire stay. His balls were the color of the deepest oceans at this point. A stiff breeze could set him off.

"I probably should have allowed you time to relieve yourself." She giggled.

"I'll be fine," he reassured her.

There was a moment of silence before she pulled her hand away from his.

"So, how long are you planning to keep up this charade? I mean, a picture on social media will blow over in a few days, weeks tops. Meeting your family? That's a whole other level of complicated."

Dom nodded. He almost wished he hadn't panicked and declared Sinai his girlfriend in front of his mother. He could have let her leave, could have let his mother think she was just a fling. They obviously weren't in the same circles, and from what he could gather about her relationship with her ex, she probably didn't have plans to stay in Mulberry much longer anyway.

"Let's talk about that after dinner with my family."

"Right," Sinai said.

They maintained casual conversation until they pulled up to her apartment building.

"Do you want me to walk you up?"

Sinai smiled and shook her head.

"No, thank you. I don't want to take up any more of your time."

Sinai was out the door before he could tell her it was no problem at all. He would love to have even just a few minutes more of her by his side. The thought scared him, so he forced himself to stay put and watch like a sad puppy as Sinai went into her building. He released a sigh. He shouldn't feel so disappointed that she seemed to be distancing herself from him already. It only made sense. Despite what happened between them, they were still strangers.

He pulled away from the curb and headed toward his shop. He needed to make sure everything was fine at Westmoore's after the storm. He'd sunk a ton of money into upgrading the shop, but the building was old, and so was much of the plumbing. On his way, he passed by a phone store, and he remembered that Sinai had broken her phone. He had her number, but what use was that if she couldn't answer. He pulled over and went inside. They were empty, and the only employee present was a young kid who looked pissed off to have to be at work when the roads were only just getting cleared.

"Can I help you?"

Dom smiled at the young man. "Yeah, my girlfriend broke her phone."

* * *

Back in her apartment, Sinai dropped her purse on her couch and headed straight for the shower. She wanted to wash the memories away. The feel of Dom's touch, the overwhelming emotions flooding her brain, all of it. She turned the spray on as hot as she could handle before stepping in. The water was almost scalding, and her body tensed at the heat before relaxing. She rubbed the back of her neck. The emotions welled up in her throat, threatening to choke her, and so she screamed, letting the tears flow and the sobs start in earnest.

She sank to the floor of the shower. Not caring that her hair was getting wet, she planned to literally wash her hair of all this mess. She would allow herself to fall apart this afternoon but, in the morning, she would wake up and get her shit together.

If she was completely honest with herself, there were worse ways she could have dealt with this break-up. Yes, she'd had strong feelings for Carter, but love had been elusive. Three years and she couldn't even say she had loved him. Not in love and yet willing to follow him, for what? The possibility that love would grow between them?

So stupid. Naïve.

Maybe because he had been her first. First lover, first adult relationship. Amayah had warned her about being clingy. For always treating relationships as forever. Sinai turned off the water, which had run cold, and grabbed a towel.

Not anymore. From now on, Sinai was going to treat all men as disposable. Starting with Dominic Westmoore. She'd finish whatever nonsense was going to unfold with him, and then she was taking a break from relationships. She needed time to be Sinai and dedicate herself to the things she loved, not men who barely gave her needs a second thought.

Determined, Sinai rushed through her hair routine. There

was no use in spending the time straightening it. She combed it and put it in four thick twists before wrapping it with her silk scarf.

Next, she went into her bedroom and slid on her favorite pajamas. As she closed the drawer, she realized there was no need for her pajamas to be in the very bottom drawer any longer. They could go in the top drawer, which she had cleaned out for Carter to use. He'd always complained about being too tall to reach so low for his things.

She pulled open the top drawer and stared at his Armani boxers and argyle socks. Anger filled her gut, and she marched into the kitchen to grab a trash bag. Step one of a break-up was to clean out all of your ex's shit. She'd already started on the emotional baggage. It was time to take care of the physical.

She cleared out the drawer, went through her things, and discarded any gifts he'd given her, which weren't very many. Next were the pictures. She didn't even bother removing them from the frames, just chucked them right into the black plastic bag. When she was done, she flopped down on her bed. His cologne wafted up from the sheets, and it turned her stomach. He'd sprayed his cologne on them so she wouldn't forget him while he was gone on his trip. She stripped her bed and shoved the sheets in the bag too.

It was time for a new set anyway. The deep blue linen hadn't fit her style, but Carter hadn't wanted to sleep on anything that quote "Would remind him of his mother."

She had never met his mother, so she had no idea if it was true her aesthetic was similar to hers. Another sign they hadn't been as serious as she thought.

Sinai set the bag by the front door. She'd toss it in the morning on her way to work. For now, she just wanted to veg out on her couch and binge-watch her favorite movies.

* * *

Dom smiled as he went up the elevator to Sinai's place. He hadn't been invited, but after being at the shop all day, he couldn't wait to see her. He didn't plan to stay, just to drop off the phone he bought for her.

The elevator dinged, signaling it had arrived at her floor. He was suddenly nervous. She had buzzed him in, so she knew he was coming, but there had been a hint of annoyance in her voice. Maybe he was too eager. That was definitely not his style. Other than Mina, he'd never really chased a woman before. The door slid open, and Sinai was standing right there, her arms crossed over her chest. She was dressed in thick fluffy pajamas, and her hair was wrapped in a scarf.

"I was planning to meet you in the lobby," she said.

"Oh, well, I'm here."

She yawned and stretched before signaling for him to follow her. She hadn't even commented on the bouquet of roses in his hand. They were obviously for her, and yet she didn't seem to even notice them. Dom noted the giant black trash bag filled to the brim sitting just inside her door. It must be all the things her ex had left at her place. The sheer amount of it told him that things had been serious between the two of them. No man left that much stuff at a woman's house unless he was confident. He would never piss her off enough to regret it.

"I don't mean to intrude. I just wanted to bring you these and maybe plan to meet up before Sunday," he said.

Sinai nodded and picked up the half-empty bottle of rose from her counter and took a swig. She didn't even look at the phone box he'd set on the counter, nor did she even look at him. She just walked over to her couch and flopped down before turning on the dance movie that had been paused on the screen.

Dom stood there awkwardly for a moment before she spoke.

"Come join me," she said and waved him over.

"Are you sure? I don't want to intrude."

Sinai groaned, and her head fell back and rolled to look at him.

"Thank you for the flowers and the concern. I'm just in a foul mood this evening and don't really feel like chatting."

Dom nodded and crossed the room to her. He sat down on the couch next to her, and she snuggled into his arms as if they were an established couple used to snuggling on the couch.

"What are we watching?"

"One of my favorite movies. If you look in the background, you can see my sister and me right there," Sinai pointed at the screen, and sure enough, there was a young Sinai and her double moving across the screen. Not that Sinai wasn't young, she was five years his junior, but she was obviously in her tweens for this scene.

"Wow, you're a movie star." He laughed.

She shook her head. "Not at all. Amayah and I won a

sweepstake for this one-time cameo in the sequel of our favorite dance movie."

"Still, a lot of people would kill for any sort of movie credit. Do you still dance?"

"Not as much as I would like."

"My sister does ballet; I can ask her what studio she goes to if you're interested."

Sinai chuckled softly and looked up at him. Her brown eyes were red and puffy as if she had spent the whole day crying. He cupped her face with his hand and held her gaze.

"Thank you, but I think it's best if I limit the chances of running into your family, you know, for after this charade is over."

The remainder of their limited time together struck Dom like a kick to the face. He let go of her and turned his attention back to the movie. He'd be lying if he said he hadn't seen it before; his sister loved to dance and had forced him to see this in theaters. It was the kind of movie that was more about the dancing than the plot.

"Speaking of, when are you free this week?"

"Thursday afternoon, I'm usually free," she said.

"Thursdays are busy for me," Dom said. "What about lunch tomorrow."

Sinai seemed to think about it for a second before nodding. "I can possibly swing that; do you know Café Yarrow?"

"Of course, it's close to my shop."

"Good, I can meet you there at 11:45?"

"Sure thing," Dom said.

He hadn't realized he was so tense about their situation until they'd confirmed their date for the following day.

He settled into her couch, and she turned her attention back to the movie. They didn't speak for the rest of the film, except to share the bottle of rose. He wasn't a rose fan, but he also didn't want to let her drink the whole bottle alone.

Sinai fell asleep in his arms before the movie finished. Her soft snoring was something he hadn't noticed at his place. Maybe it was the wine, or maybe the fact she'd obviously been wallowing in grief over her ex. Just the thought of that man made Dom enraged. If he ever got that man alone, he would...

"Dom," Sinai's soft whimper as she rubbed her cheek against his lap cut off his train of thought. "Mmmm," she moaned and rolled over onto her back.

The way her lips parted and her brow furrowed, Dom knew she was having a sex dream, and apparently, he was in it. He'd recognize her subtle orgasm face anywhere after the tryst they had.

Sinai reached her hand up to her breast and gave it a squeeze. She bit her bottom lip and whimpered again. Her back arched, and then she stilled and sat straight up. "Fuck!" she cried out.

"Good dream?"

Sinai leaped off the couch with a shriek. "Oh my God! Did we? Were you?"

Dom held up his hands. "I promise I didn't touch you. You fell asleep on my lap."

Sinai groaned and sank back down to the couch, but he noticed she chose to do so on the opposite side of the couch from him. She brought her knees up under her chin and wrapped her arms around them.

"You're tired. I should get going," Dom said and quickly

moved toward the door. He knew that if he stayed any longer, he would be overstaying his welcome.

"Dom, wait."

He paused at the door and turned to look at her. If she asked him to stay, he would. If she asked him to stay, he would surely fuck her senseless, and the look in her eyes told him she knew that to be a fact. She licked her lips, and he waited. He waited for her to say the words. He could see the lust in her eyes, the need. He felt it too.

"Thank you, I'll see you tomorrow."

And there it was, what he hadn't wanted to hear but knew was for the best. He nodded and let himself out.

* * *

Sinai growled in frustration as she kicked and pouted like a toddler. What was wrong with her? Why had she let him go? Because you don't need the added complication of having him fuck the life out of you.

Sinai got up and went to the kitchen counter where he had left the roses he'd brought her. She picked up the bouquet and sniffed them. They were fragrant and bright red. He had to have spent a grip to get such beautiful fresh roses in the middle of winter and just after Valentine's Day. Sinai didn't have a vase, but she did have a glass lemonade pitcher that would make do. It wasn't until she was filling the pitcher with water that she noticed the box on the counter next to the flowers. She set the pitcher down and reached for the box, her heart swelled, and tears fell from her eyes. He'd bought her a new phone, the latest model of the phone she owned. It had just come out a few days ago. Excited, she opened the box and followed the activation procedures. He'd been thoughtful enough to have purchased an unlocked version, so she had no problem with transferring her number and content from her back up.

She finished placing the flowers in the pitcher and snapped a quick selfie of herself with them before sending Dom a thank you text. He had conveniently tucked his contact information in the note with the flowers.

She really had been feeling like shit when he arrived, but now, she felt better. She felt cared for. She wandered into her bedroom and climbed into bed with a smile on her face. Maybe pretending to be Dom's girlfriend wasn't going to be so bad after all. If he continued to treat her like this, she would definitely have a standard for her next foray into a romantic relationship, when she was ready, of course.

Hips moved smoothly from left to right, Sinai let the rhythm of the music drive the movement of her body. Dance had always been her way to relieve stress, yet ever since Dom had dropped by her place last night, she hadn't been able to focus on anything but him and how sweet he was to her. Even now, as she danced, her song of choice was about steamy forbidden nights and sappy love songs instead of her usual hip hop faves. Hell, she was at the dance studio early just because of last night and the reminder that it had been a while since she'd indulged in her favorite pastime.

He'd offered to get a recommendation for a studio from his sister, for fuck's sake. How sweet could a man be? She hadn't needed the recommendation. However, one of the first things Sinai had done when she moved was find a studio that she could use with her odd schedule. She paid a monthly fee like anyone would with a gym. She occasionally took drop-in classes, but this last year she'd been so focused on Carter and his needs that she'd stopped coming as often as she had before.

She could feel the lack of practice in the burn of her muscles and the lack of flexibility. How had she managed to let herself go so easily?

The music stopped briefly as her phone began to buzz. It was Amayah, no doubt wanting an update since Sinai hadn't called her as she promised.

"Good, you're alive, so I can fucking kill you for making me worry about you!"

Sinai smiled and shook her head.

"Sorry, I broke my phone."

"IS that some new slang for getting your back blown out by tall, dark, and handsome because your phone doesn't sound broken to me."

Sinai grabbed her towel and wiped the sweat from her brow.

"I did not have sex with him, for one. Two, I did break my phone, but Dom replaced it for me."

Amayah tsked. "Girl, no dude buys you a new phone if he didn't already get the goods."

"I'm not saying things didn't happen, but he mostly just watched," Sinai replied.

"Watched? Girl, I had no idea you were into some kinky shit. Anyway, I'm glad you aren't dead and chopped up in a sewer somewhere. Don't make me worry about you like this again. I gotta run. I just got to work."

Amayah hung up before Sinai could say anything more. Sinai took a gulp of water before collecting her things. After checking the time, she was already behind schedule for getting to work on time. Her normally long shower after a dance session would have to be cut to a quick five-minute rinse.

Sinai rushed to the locker room and was just about to head to the showers when she ran headfirst into Holly. She was one of the dance instructors that Sinai had taken classes with. "Sinai! Long time no see!"

"Hi, Holly, I would love to chat, but I'm going to be late for work," Sinai said.

Holly smiled. "No worries. I'll see you in class, tonight right?"

Sinai nodded in the affirmative before stepping into the shower stall. She didn't think twice about it until she collapsed into her office chair, and her phone buzzed with a reminder email from the studio. Holly had signed her up for the class, an obvious and not so subtle hint that she had, in fact, been missed in the small adult hip-hop class.

She was going to have a busy day indeed between the little fires that were sure to have cropped up with her pending events, her date with Dom, and now a dance class after work. She would be too busy and exhausted to worry about anything but what was right in front of her. She turned on her computer and got to work checking her emails and messaging vendors to make sure the blizzard hadn't cost any catastrophic delays.

Working at an event planning company hadn't been Sinai's dream, but it paid the bills and allowed her to get to know Mulberry.

Emails didn't take too long, so she moved on to the stack of contracts that Benjamin had left on her desk just as she'd come in that morning. Benjamin was the boss's assistant and was always the first to arrive, rain, sleet, or snow.

She wished she had his zest for the job, but at least she wasn't on the floor as the main planners liked to call it. She got to stay in her cubicle and handle the paperwork, which was fine with her. She thrived in spaces that she could control and event planning on the ground floor was anything but controllable.

Maybe that was Sinai's problem. She needed too much control in everything but her relationships. A smile touched her lips as she thought about Dom and just how much control she'd had over him. He'd followed her every whim, and yet she had felt so out of control, it was exhilarating.

"Someone's cheery today!"

Sinai looked up from the contracts she was supposed to be checking. Her coworker, and office gossip, Monica, was standing over her with a knowing look on her face.

Sinai flushed as she realized she'd just been caught daydreaming on the job. It was completely unlike her, and Monica wouldn't hesitate to spread the news as soon as she left Sinai's cubicle.

"I guess I just woke up on the right side of the bed this morning." Sinai shrugged.

"Dominic Westmoore's side of the bed, I presume," Monica sighed and winked at Sinai, "what I wouldn't give to take a bite out of that gorgeous hunk of chocolate, girl, you have to give me details."

Sinai laughed, a harsh edge to her voice. She usually didn't mind Monica's penchant for gossip. She was so well tapped into the rumor mill that she alone brought in 30% of the clients to the firm. Yet, today with Monica snooping for gossip about Dom, Sinai wasn't going to play along. The last thing she needed was to add any more fuel to the gossip mill fires about her and Dom.

"My bed, Monica. I woke up alone in my bed."

"Oh, I see! It was a blizzard bae situation for real. I figured, no offense, but Dominic Westmoore is way out of your league, love."

With that, Monica flounced away, and Sinai resisted the urge to flip her off.

Not Dom's type? Sinai had never considered the thought. Hell, she wasn't even considering Dom. What business did she have worrying about his type or not?

Frustrated with the turn of her mood, Sinai dove into work.

* * *

Dom checked his watch after he sent the waitress at Café Yarrow away for the third time. It was 12:15, and Sinai was nowhere to be seen. Anger and disappointment warred inside of him. Dom wasn't used to being stood up. He pulled out his phone and checked his messages. There was nothing new from Sinai, only the adorable picture of her posing with the flowers he brought her last night. He felt like he was in a Katy Perry video. Sinai was hot and then cold. She'd said yes to this date, but her action was telling him no. For a moment, Dom was slightly more upset that he even knew that much about Katy Perry and that he even knew about her at all. Pop music wasn't usually on his radar but having a little sister meant he knew things a grown-ass black man usually avoided.

When 12:20 rolled around, he signaled the waiter to order to go. He had an appointment at 1, and he wasn't about to be humiliated a second longer. At least Café Yarrow was a safe restaurant. People who frequented here minded their own damn business.

He walked the short distance back to his shop. West-moore's was an institution in Mulberry. One of the first black barbershops in the city and now the oldest, Westmoore's had grown from a small mom and pop establishment to a hot spot and rite of passage for men of influence in the area. Athletes, politicians, and famous musicians all frequented the establishment alongside those whose families had been customers from the very establishment of the shop by Dom's Great, great, great grandfather.

The proudest day of his life was when he'd been given the keys to this place by his grandfather. While Dom's grandfather had worked a chair while he was in college, his heart had never been in the old place, and neither had his father's. It was a miracle at all that the place was still open. Dom's grandfather had grander ambitions and had helped to bolster not just the family's wealth but their status as part of the elite in the community. Dom's father had taken to the family's marketing business as well.

Dom had the prerogative to keep both family legacies alive and well. So, while he worked and ran Westmoore's Barber Shop, he was also acted as the face of the family.

Sinai, of course, knew nothing about this, and at this point, it had to be intentional. A simple internet search would have clued her in, but she didn't seem to want to learn more about him, especially after standing him up for the lunch date.

The shop was full as usual, appointments needed to be booked months in advance for newcomers, and there were plenty who were dying to get their hair cut in such a hallowed establishment. Dom's client today was the next candidate for governor. He was flying in from the capital just to get his hair cut for the announcement of his candidacy. Dom needed to get his head right before he was going to put anything sharp near that man's head.

Just stepping into the shop and smelling the familiar scent of his family's signature aftershave was enough to bolster his mood just a little.

He was instantly met with a plethora of greetings ranging from "Hey, man to Sup, Dom."

He nodded at the customers as he passed, but he couldn't bring himself to smile. He was still pissed about Sinai standing him up and even more pissed that he cared so much about it, about her.

He made his way to the back of the shop and sat down at the employee break table to scarf down his food and get ready for his client. The familiar routine of lining up all his tools and prepping his space eased him, and by the time the gubernatorial candidate showed up, Dom was ready for action.

He greeted the man with a smile and introduced himself before ushering him into the chair to begin what Dom imagined was the best haircut experience the man would ever have in his life if he didn't become a regular.

* * *

"Shit!" Sinai cursed as she was informed by the hostess that Dom had already left.

It was her fault; she'd gotten caught up in work, and she had been stupid to think he'd still be waiting for her after 1 p.m. for a date they scheduled for just before noon. She bit her lip and thanked the woman before heading back down the staircase that led to the rooftop restaurant.

She pulled out her phone to send him a message but couldn't think of the right way to express her very deep and very real regret.

If she had been paying attention to the time, one, she wouldn't have stood him up, or at least she could have texted him that she wasn't going to show or that something had come up. She let out a frustrated groan as she got to the bottom of the stairs.

Maybe she should call him instead, though he probably wouldn't answer her calls after this either. Then she remembered he'd told her his shop was just down the street. She had no idea what his shop was, but she figured if she walked down the street, maybe she would be able to figure it out.

She headed in one direction and immediately felt stupid. She pulled out her phone and called her sister.

"We were supposed to meet for lunch, and I stood him up," she said as soon as Amayah answered.

"Nai! What are you playing at? I thought this was just a blizzard bae?"

"It's a bit more complicated than that. I mean, he bought me flowers and a phone. I don't plan to date him, date him like for real, but you know, be courteous."

Amayah snorted. "You're already failing at this, Sinai."

"I know, and now I'm stuck. Like I don't want him to think I stood him up on purpose, but I can't think of what to say that would really convey what I'm feeling, and so now I'm wandering the cold-ass streets looking for his shop."

"Oh lord, girl, have you even searched this man?"

"No?"

"Nai! I know more about this man than you do, and you spent time in his fucking bed not having sex. Look, hang up and look him up."

"Fine!" Sinai hung up and was just about to search him on the internet when she looked up and saw the sign that said Westmoore's Barbershop. It couldn't be a coincidence. She tucked her phone away and took a deep breath. Shaking out her nerves, she put on a brave face and opened the door.

She was met with immediate silence as about twenty pairs of male eyes swiveled in her direction.

"Can I help you?" a man toward the back asked.

Sinai bit her lip, her nerves threatening to get to her.

"Uh, yeah. I'm looking for Dom?"

The man smirked and shook his head.

"Sorry, ma'am. Dom isn't available right now."

The way he said the words told her she wasn't the first woman to come to the shop looking for Dom, which further disturbed her.

"Um, okay, can you tell him Sinai stopped by."

"Sure thing," the man said and turned back to his work.

Sinai turned to leave; she had a feeling he wasn't going to say shit to Dom, except another thirst bucket came by to chat. Her hand was just on the door when Dom's familiar timber drifted from the back of the shop. She turned, and he was shaking hands with a man who obviously had just finished getting his hair cut. Her eyes drifted over Dom in his black t-shirt and thigh-hugging slacks.

He bid the man farewell, and as he watched the man leave, his eyes met with hers. The jovial look on his face died, and she froze, unsure of if she should rush to him and apologize or rush out the door.

"Excuse me," his customer said to her.

"Oh, sorry," she apologized and stepped aside. The man looked up at her, and a bright grin spread on his face.

"Blizzard Bae! I knew you looked familiar."

Sinai's mouth fell open. She knew the story had made it online, and Monica was a gossipmonger, so she wasn't surprised he had seen it, but this man in front of her looked vaguely like a politician she'd seen on tv. Nothing like a man who would read trashy gossip.

A whisper went around the room as the men looked from Sinai to Dom and back.

Dom cleared his throat and marched over to Sinai.

"Best of luck on your campaign, man," Dom said and practically shoved the man out the door before grabbing Sinai's arm and dragging her to the back of the shop. He didn't stop until they were alone in what Sinai imagined was the employee break room.

"What are you doing here, Sinai," Dom snapped.

She wasn't used to the sharpness of his tongue, and she looked down at the floor. "I just came to apologize for missing our lunch date," she said.

"Don't worry about it. It wasn't like it was a real date or anything. Just don't be late for Sunday. Waste my time once is all you get," he said.

She looked up, and fire danced in his eyes.

He was hurt. She could see it in the set of his jaw, the almost pout of his lips.

"Dom, I'm sorry. I really am. I didn't mean to leave you hanging like that."

"Like I said. Don't be late for Sunday. Now, if you'll excuse me, this is my place of business. I need to get back to work."

He brushed past her, opened the door, and leaned against the frame waiting for her to leave first.

Sinai may have been nervous before, but now she was pissed. He would not dismiss her like this like she was nothing. She slid her body up against his and pressed a soft kiss to his cheek before whispering in his ear, "You're so sexy when you pout like a child."

She pulled away and took one step before he was pulling her back and into his arms. He crushed his mouth to hers, and she melted into him, wrapping her arms around his neck. A not-so-subtle cough broke into their kiss, and Dom pulled away.

"Sunday, don't forget," he said and let her go.

Sinai smirked and shook her head. "How could I forget dinner with your family?" she said before walking away with a slightly exaggerated sway to her hips, she could feel the heat of his gaze on her ass and thighs, and that soothed the sting of his earlier words.

* * *

Jay shook his head at Dom, and if they weren't in his place of business, Dom would have flipped him the bird.

"Never thought I'd see the day," Jay said.

"What?"

"The Day the great Dom fell. Blizzard bae, huh." Jay chuckled.

Dom was willing to go along with Jay's teasing; they were good friends, and Jay was one of Dom's best employees. Yet, hearing that name in reference to Sinai didn't sit right with him.

"Don't call my girlfriend that. Her name is Sinai."

"Wow, the G-word, and she's meeting your family? Yo, if you want to save me time and money on a tux, you and Bechet can have a double wedding."

This time Dom did flip him off before going to prep his space for his next client. The teasing from his employees didn't stop for the rest of the night, and Dom, despite his better judgment, couldn't help but play along as if Sinai really were his. After all, she was gorgeous, talented, and sexy as hell. There was obvious chemistry between them. Just now wasn't the time. Again, thoughts of her ex intruded on his happy thoughts of Sinai. He had no idea if she'd even spoken to him since that first night. She seemed to be actively trying to get over him, but that didn't mean she'd informed the bastard of her plans.

He pulled out his phone and started to message her about it but changed his mind. It wasn't his business. No, his time was much better spent on figuring out a way to keep Sinai around after Sunday.

* * *

Sweat dripped from Sinai's body in buckets. She hadn't worked this hard in a long time. Holly's class hadn't been the usual hip hop aerobics. It had been the advanced dance class, which was mostly attended by the studio's competition team. Sinai had been surprised at how well she'd kept up with them, given her lack of conditioning. Still, she knew she wasn't on their level. Holly came up to her with a big smile on her face.

"You did great!"

Sinai rolled her eyes. "I'm so out of shape, I'm dying!"

Holly laughed. "You're just out of practice. Trust me, a month of this class, and you'll be right in with the rest of the team."

"I'm not a competition dancer."

"You are now!" Holly said and tossed her the black team shirt.

The members of the team who had been milling around and chatting after class gathered around her and started welcoming her to the team. She knew she should be more forceful with turning down the offer to be on the team, but part of her didn't want to. She'd watched them for over a year now, and she couldn't say she wasn't envious. Hell, she would definitely have more time now that Carter was out of the picture. What was the harm in taking a chance on something she enjoyed?

She was so caught up in the excitement the next thing she knew, she was at a dance club with them, drinking and partying on a Tuesday night. This was definitely not something she'd done since freshman year of college. She stumbled into her apartment sometime around 2 a.m.

At least the dancing kept her from getting too drunk. All she had to worry about was her entire body being sore the next day. Hell, it was sore now, something similar to the delicious soreness she felt after her marathon self-gratification at Dom's.

Heat flooded her body at the thought of him watching as she stripped out her clothes. She stood naked in front of her full-length mirror and touched herself, watching herself like he had watched her. Mimicking the tick in his jaw as he got rock hard and was trying not to touch himself at her command. Yet, it wasn't the same. She picked up her phone and sent him an invite for a video chat. He probably wouldn't answer; it was late and a weeknight. She continued to touch herself while she waited and was surprised when not only did he accept her request, but he was calling her.

"I knew you were touching yourself," he said sleepily as soon as his video popped on the screen.

"I thought it only fair I let you watch since I was such a naughty girl earlier." She tilted the camera so he could see her touching herself between her legs.

"Beautiful, baby. You're glistening like liquid diamonds."

Sinai moaned as more arousal coated her fingers. Just as she thought, having him talk to her, having him watch her even if it wasn't in person was exactly what she needed to get off.

"Slow down, baby. I want you to savor the feel of your pussy, and when you cum, I want you to open those pretty lips wide, so I can see your muscles fluttering like a sexy little butterfly."

"Too late," Sinai cried, thrusting her fingers deep. She spread them wide so he could get the view he requested.

"Damn, Sinai. I need to get in that pussy. I love watching, don't get me wrong, but my dick is granite hard right now."

Sinai brought the phone up to her face. "Touch yourself, Dom. I want to watch you cum all over your sheets."

"As you wish, Madame."

He lowered the camera until she had a full view of his

thick chocolate bar. He gave a whole new meaning to thicker than a snicker. Sinai wasn't usually a fan of nuts in her chocolate, but if given a chance, she'd swallow every bit of the nut from his. She watched how he gripped himself. How he slid his hands up and down, stroking himself.

"Fuck I get why watching makes you so hard. I swear I'm going to orgasm just watching you stroke that cock."

His hand pumped faster, fingertips dancing over the tip of him with each stroke, spreading his glistening precum over his shaft. Sinai licked her lips and moaned; she gripped her sheets to keep from touching herself. It was only fair she denied herself while he got his. It was a turn of play.

"Mmm, damn it, Dom. How am I supposed to keep that out of my pussy the next time I see you? It's so lickable, so rideable. Fuck!"

Her curse came in unison with jets of pearly white spurt from his tip all over his thighs and sheets, the drizzles of white contrasting against his thigh like the ultimate erotic art.

"Goodnight, Dom." Sinai hung up before things got awkward. She sank her fingers into her pussy and came instantly before letting herself drift off to sleep.

6

"Are you sure this is alright?" Sinai checked her reflection for what felt like the millionth time.

Amayah scoffed on the other end of the video call.

"You look absolutely stunning. Remember, there is no need for you to be nervous. It's not like you're meeting the family, meeting the family. This is just step one to getting on with your life."

Sinai was sure Amayah meant for her words to be reassuring, but they weren't. If anything, they made her even more nervous. What if they hated her? Would Dom take the opportunity to end things right then and there? That would be the simplest solution, but the idea of being discarded again so soon after Carter hit her right in her gut. On the other hand, if they liked her, if they loved her, it would make it that much harder for her and Dom to make a clean break. They would have questions, so many questions. Of course, that would be on Dom to explain not her, but also in her line of work being persona non grata with one of the most influential families in the area would be career suicide.

"Oh my God, Nai! I can see the steam coming out of your ears from overthinking this. Listen, just be yourself, don't worry about anything else."

Sinai let out an exasperated sigh and smoothed imaginary wrinkles from the red sundress she'd chosen for the evening. It was casual enough to seem like she wasn't trying too hard but fancy enough that she wouldn't be out of place if the dinner was a more formal affair. Dom had assured her casual would be fine, but she wasn't going to take a chance on it.

"Okay, I'm fine. I've got this. Dom should be here any minute." Sinai blew a kiss to her sister before hanging up.

She checked the time and grabbed her purse. Dom was picking her up, and she was going to wait in the lobby. It would help her not to chicken out and fain sick. Despite her better judgment, Sinai had to look up the Westmoore's and had cursed the universe for sending her toppling into Dom Westmoore of all people. If things went too south with him and his family, she would definitely have to move.

Speaking of moving, her lease was almost up. Maybe she should just cut her losses and go home. She could crash with her parents until she found another job, or maybe she'd go and stay with her sister in Sowell City. Amayah had told her all sorts of interesting tales about the city.

The sound of the buzzer cut off her train of thought. She rushed to the door and pressed the call button.

"Hey, Dom. I'll be right down!"

She didn't wait for his reply, just grabbed her purse and keys and headed for the elevator. When she got to the ground floor, her smile dropped instantly. It wasn't Dom waiting for her. It was Carter. He was dressed in his usual off-the-clock look of a pullover and jeans.

"You're looking nice," he said, but there was no sincerity in his voice. His face was set in a stern, disapproving look as his gaze raked her body.

Sinai suddenly felt self-conscious and uncomfortable. Any confidence in her look being appropriate fled with the closing of the elevator door behind her.

"I have plans," she said, disappointed in the defeated tone of her voice.

"I heard, with Dom? I'll wait with you. I'd love to meet the man you chose to debase yourself with."

His words were like a slap in the face, but instead of being hurt by them, she was enraged.

"How dare you?"

"I should be asking you that. I get if you were mad about my trip over the holiday, but you could have just told me. What you did was, wow. I would expect something like that from your loose-ass sister but not from you."

"Fuck you, Carter. Oh wait, I'm sorry your secretary has already handled that."

He looked stricken for a moment before he recovered.

"Is that what this is about? You thought I was fucking Michelle just because she was on the trip with me?"

"I don't think. I saw your ass with your tongue down her throat. I came to surprise you before your flight, but apparently, I was the one who was in for a surprise."

"I never knew you had such an active imagination. Maybe you should have used that in the bedroom instead of to hallucinate some out-of-character shit."

Sinai pinched the bridge of her nose. She wasn't going to keep arguing with Carter. There was no point. She was done with him. She'd trashed his shit and blocked him on social media and from her phone. He was a no factor.

"I know what I saw. I'm not an idiot, and I sure as hell am not going to stand for any more of your disrespect. Goodbye, Carter."

Sinai pushed past him and out of the lobby. Thankfully Dom was just rounding his car toward the building. The way his jaw dropped at the sight of her sent a thrill through her and lifted her spirits. Dom caught her in his arms, and she stood on tiptoe to press a kiss to his lips. He didn't hesitate to return the kiss, his large hands gripping her back and pressing her flush against his body.

"Well, hello to you too, beautiful," he said, breaking their kiss.

Dom held her away from him and guided her into a spin. "Is this okay?"

"More than okay. I'm glad you met me down here; otherwise, I would have had to call my mother and beg off."

"Oh no! I am not about to get on your mother's bad side."

"Fucking, slut!" Carter's voice cut into her bubble of joy with Dom.

Dom's jovial smile turned deadly as he positioned Sinai behind him.

"What the fuck did you just say?"

Carter smirked before walking right up to Dom. "I didn't stutter. Enjoy the cheating bitch."

Sinai lunged for Carter, but Dom held her back at the same time he swung and hit Carter himself. Carter stumbled back from the force of the blow and tripped over his own feet before falling to the ground.

"Disrespect my girl again and see what happens," Dom spat before shuffling Sinai quickly into his car.

"So that was your ex," Dom said, gripping the steering wheel so tight his knuckles were white.

"I'm sorry. He just showed up. I thought once I told him we were done, he would just move on."

Dom laughed harshly. "Nah, a douche like him is territorial as fuck. He may cheat, but he sees you as his possession. He won't let go of you that easy."

Sinai bit her lip. If she thought about it, Carter had shown possessive tendencies. The one time she had even thought of taking a break from him, he'd thrown such a fit about her not caring enough about him that she'd scrapped the idea.

"It doesn't matter. I'm done with him. I've already blocked him and removed him from my life. He will just have to get over it and move on."

Dom reached over and took her hand in his.

"After dinner, come stay at my place for the night."

"I don't think that will be necessary. He won't come back after you knocked him on his ass."

"I wasn't asking because of him," he said and kissed her fingertips.

She sucked in a breath as his tongue flicked out to lave the pad of her thumb.

"Oh," she gasped, and he chuckled.

"Is that a yes?"

"I'll make up my mind after dinner."

* * *

Dom focused on the sway of Sinai's hips in that sexy ass

sundress to keep his mind off of killing her ex. The man had only further proven to Dom that he was nothing more than a selfish little boy who didn't know how rare a jewel-like Sinai truly was.

It had only been a week, and Dom wasn't sure how he would ever let her go. He was enthralled with her. She was the treasure, and he was the mighty dragon desperate to get his claws deep enough to keep her by his side.

"I just realized we never really talked about how we met," Sinai said just as she was about to open the front door.

Dom sighed. She was right, but it was too late to come up with something now. Dom wasn't the best liar, and the only reason he'd got away with telling people Sinai was his girl was because, despite his better judgment, that's exactly what she was to him. She was his. He just needed to give her the time and space to realize that she wanted him to be hers as well.

"We'll tell them the truth. We ran into each other on the street and connected after I returned your purse. We just won't tell them it was the night of the blizzard."

He opened the door and was immediately greeted by Alicia.

"Oh my God, mom told me you were bringing blizzard bae!"

"Alicia," Dom warned.

She ignored him and looped her arm with Sinai's.

"I love your dress. How did you two meet?"

And so the night began. Alicia stayed glued to Sinai's side the rest of the evening. At first, she was just introducing her to the rest of his family, and he had a small window of opportunity to snag Sinai's attention while Alicia had been ordered to help bring the dishes to the table. Only for his bastard little brother to monopolize her time chatting her up about her job as an event planner. A detail he hadn't even known about her.

Then dinner was served, and he finally got a chance to be close to her again. He placed his hand on her thigh under the table, and she looked up at him, humor and a hint of lust in her eyes. She leaned close to him and whispered in his ear, "Careful now. Your family is watching us closely," she said.

Dom cupped her chin and pressed a kiss to her lips. "Then we should really sell the show," he whispered back.

He got lost in the feel of her soft lips and forgot that he was, in fact, in front of his family until a napkin ring caught him in the side of the head.

"Hey, now! Save all that for after dinner," his father said.

Sinai flushed with embarrassment, but Dom just sat back with a smug grin on his face. If he'd been worried about his family not approving of Sinai, the fact that they hadn't put on pretenses within the first ten minutes of their arrival told him they most certainly approved.

"Sinai, I saw on your Instagram that you are a dancer!" Alicia gushed as she brought out their mother's famous apple pie for dessert.

"It's a hobby," Sinai said with a shrug.

Alicia's mouth dropped open before she fished out her phone and shoved a video of Sinai dancing alone in a studio in everyone's faces.

"That kind of extension does not come from just a hobbyist. Trust me. I'd kill for that kind of flexibility."

Sinai smiled brightly and shook her head.

"All you need is practice. Dom mentioned you take ballet?"

Alicia nodded, but she didn't seem too enthusiastic about it, which was a first. Normally, Alicia was the first to start running her mouth about how she was the best dancer in her class, how she got all the solos and made all the other girls jealous. That was concerning.

"Ballet is nice, but sometimes I wish I could do something with more freedom."

Sinai looked to Dom as if he could provide her with a clue on how to respond. He had no idea. Alicia had always been into anything that pertained to dance, but he realized Ballet had been their mother's idea.

"Well, maybe we can meet up one day and just dance, no rules, just us and the music."

Alicia's smile brightened immediately.

"Of course!" she gushed before turning to Dom and giving him the stink eye.

"Don't you dare break up with her before I get a chance to dance," she pouted.

Dom shook his head. "You think I'd even bring her here if I was going to break up with her?"

Sinai nudged him in his side before turning a smile on his sister. "Don't worry. Even if Dom proves to be a complete idiot for letting me go, I promise not to hold it against you. I'm a woman of my word."

Alicia smiled and stuck her tongue out at him before sitting down and waiting for her piece of the pie.

* * *

Sinai had loved almost every minute with Dom and his family. All her fears had been for not. They were the least pretentious people of influence she had ever met. Sinai could see where Dom got his gentle nature and manners from. The only hitch to the evening was Dom declaring that he had no plans of breaking up with her. The implied never was there even if he hadn't said it.

Still, despite her own misgivings, she had faltered in that aspect as well, promising not only to meet up with his sister for a dance session but also agreeing to a tea with his mother the following week. Her actions were not that of a woman not interested in continuing a relationship with a man she barely even knew.

"You okay over there?" Dom asked.

They were in his car headed to her place. He hadn't brought up her staying with him that evening, and now away from the welcoming glow of his family, she knew it was probably for the best that she kept her distance from now on.

"Yes, I was just thinking about how I'm going to break it to your mother that we've split."

Dom cleared his throat. "We don't need to think about that now. We can give it a few weeks. Give everyone time to get over the excitement."

Sinai nodded and stared out the window at the passing buildings.

"But we should talk about it soon."

Dom sighed and took her hand in his. "Let's just drop it for now. We'll swing by your place so you can grab your things to stay overnight, and then we'll head to my place."

Sinai pulled her hand out of his grasp. "Actually, I'm pretty tired. I think I'll just stay home tonight."

Dom didn't say a word to her for the rest of the car ride.

It was the first time that things between them had felt this tense and awkward. She much preferred when he'd raged and pouted at her like when she had stood him up. This silent, emotionless wall Dom had put up was too much even for her.

It's better this way, Nai. Don't let yourself get caught up.

When Dom pulled up to her place, she was so ready to get out of the car he hadn't even fully parked before she was out the door and headed into her building.

"Sinai!" Dom called, following her. She didn't stop. She ran into the lobby and made sure the door was closed so he couldn't follow.

She sagged against the elevator walls as the door closed her off from the view of him cursing at the front door to the lobby. She grabbed her chest and rubbed the spot that began to ache when she realized that this was probably the end. She would meet with his sister and his mother and tell them they had parted ways. It was the best course of action. The only course of action if she was going to save herself from further heartbreak.

By the time the elevator opened on her floor, Sinai felt sick to her stomach, and her eyes burned with tears. She was so distraught she belatedly realized the door to her apartment was wide open when it should have been closed and locked.

She froze in the entryway as she stood dumbfounded. Nothing seemed out of place except the bouquet of roses Dom had brought her earlier that week. Instead of on the kitchen counter, the vase she had purchased for them was smashed to pieces on the floor next to the slightly wilted blooms.

She slowly backed out of the apartment and ran for the stairs. The elevator had already gone back down, and she didn't want to chance waiting for it to come back. She took the stairs two at a time, bursting into the lobby. Her heart rate only slowed when she was safely in Dom's arms.

"Sinai, Sinai! What happened? What's wrong, baby."

"Someone broke into my apartment," she managed to get out.

"Okay, okay. Go wait in the car. I'll call the police."

He ushered her into the car while he called for the authorities. Only he hadn't dialed 9-11; apparently, a man like him had friends on the force. Powerful friends. He called the commissioner directly. Within five minutes, two nondescript black sedans pulled up behind Dom's car, and the pair of cops introduced themselves as detectives. One set stayed with her to take her statement while the other two checked out her place.

"Is there anyone who might wish you harm, Ms. Carlisle?" the detective asked her after she told them what she'd found when she came home.

Sinai shook her head.

"No, I don't really know anyone here."

Dom shook his head and pulled the other detective aside. She could hear him telling them about the altercation with Carter earlier that day. Reluctantly, Sinai gave the detectives Carter's information. They made Dom aware that even if Carter was guilty of the break-in, he could still be liable for assault.

"I could give a flying fuck about that. I just want him far away from my girlfriend," Dom said.

"Ms. Carlisle can file a restraining order against Mr. French at the precinct, but for tonight it would be best if she had a safe place to stay until we can have a talk with Mr. French."

"She's staying with me," Dom said.

The female detective looked at Sinai for confirmation, and Sinai nodded. What other choice did she have, waste her studio fee money on a hotel room for the night, and still not feel safe?

"I will be staying with Dom," she confirmed, "Is it okay if I grab a few of my things, or do I need to wait?"

"It should be alright for you to get what you need. We also ask that you check and make sure nothing is missing or otherwise out of place. If it is, don't touch it and inform us immediately."

The detective handed Sinai her card before joining her partner in discussion with the other two detectives.

"I'll come with you," Dom said.

Sinai nodded. Even knowing nothing was lurking in the shadows for her, she didn't want to be alone. Dom kept a close but respectful distance away from Sinai as she packed an overnight bag.

* * *

Dom didn't know what the hell he was feeling. He was angry, he was scared, he was heartbroken, yet hopeful. Nothing about this last week made any sense. Yet here he was with Sinai in his car on the way to his home like he originally planned but definitely not the way he had planned. He had wanted to bring her home and seduce her, to use their attraction to spur the conversation he knew they needed to have. Only now, he couldn't do that. He couldn't even touch her as she sat in the seat beside him, unshed tears glistening in her eyes.

"I can accompany you to the station tomorrow," he offered.

"Okay," she said, barely above a whisper.

"I know a few people in the security business. I can have them come wire a new system for you as well," he said.

"No need, my lease is up next month. I'll just find a new place to stay."

"I know a good realtor," he began, but Sinai slapped her hand over his mouth.

"Shut up, Dom. Stop making this harder!"

Dom used one hand to peel hers from his lips. "I'm just trying to help."

"That's the problem. You helping me all the time. You don't even know me."

"You're upset, Sinai. I'll stop talking for now," Dom said, and they rode the rest of the way to his place in tense silence.

It wasn't an unproductive silence, though, as he tried to figure out what the hell she meant about him making things harder for her. What was hard about accepting his help? What was so hard about allowing a man to treat her the way she deserved to be treated?

He pulled his car into the garage and escorted Sinai through his workshop and into his place.

"You can take the guest room," he said, but instead of disappearing into the room she'd stayed in during the blizzard, she followed him to his.

"I don't want to be alone," she said when he raised a questioning eyebrow at her.

He sighed and gestured for her to come in. They didn't speak as they changed into pajamas and then climbed into bed. She snuggled close to him, and he held her tight to his chest.

"Why is it hard to accept my help?"

Sinai sat up and stared at him. "This was supposed to be a fake relationship, Dom. A means to an end. I'm not in the right headspace for a relationship, and although I know you don't have feelings for me, you are genuinely just a good guy helping out a poor little girl like me. I just…"

"Just what, Sinai."

"I'm getting confused about what's real and what's not. When you kiss me when you look at me sometimes. I can't tell if you're just a really good actor or if I'm just projecting my own feelings on you."

Dom sat up at that, a smile on his lips. "Are you saying you have a crush on me?"

Sinai groaned and fell back, covering her face with her hands.

"I don't know, maybe, and I know I shouldn't. It doesn't make any sense, and even if the feelings are real, is it because you're fucking hot as shit and pamper me like I'm already yours, or am I just desperate to feel wanted after what Carter did to me?"

"Does it matter?"

She dropped her hands and frowned at him. "Hell, yes, it does! I'm already embarrassed by even admitting this to you, but I had to say it. I had to get it out there because if you're going to knock me on my ass, I rather it be now while I still have a chance at pretending this last week meant nothing."

Dom grabbed Sinai's ankle and pulled her under him.

"Sinai Carlisle, I've been asking myself these same questions all damn week. I know that it doesn't make sense and that it is quite possibly the worst timing in all of creation, but I am willing to wait for you. I've been scheming this whole time, trying to figure out how to get you to stay in my orbit. I have feelings for you that I shouldn't, given our circumstances."

"Are you asking me to be your girlfriend for real? I can't honestly say yes to that right now."

"No, that isn't what I'm asking. I'm asking you to be my not so platonic roommate while we both figure shit out."

Sinai laughed.

"Roommate? Really?"

"You said you were looking for a place to stay. I've got the extra space both down the hall or right here in my bed, whatever you choose."

Sinai grabbed the back of his head and pulled him down to kiss her.

"I must be insane for agreeing to such a crazy proposal."

"So, is that a yes?"

Sinai wrapped her long legs around him and nodded.

"I guess it is, but I have one condition."

"Anything you wish, Madame," Dom said, trailing kisses along her collar bone.

"No sex until we figure out what this really is about."

Dom pulled back and laughed. "No sex as in no sexual activity at all or just no penis in vagina action."

"I can't believe you just said penis and vagina action."

"I can't believe you wrapped those sexy ass legs around me only to say I can't bury my dick between them."

Sinai pouted and bat her eyelashes at him. "Please, Dom," she pleaded.

Dom rolled over onto his side and tucked the blankets tightly between them before draping his arm across her waist and pulling her against him.

"Kissing and hugging only," he grumbled.

"That is not what I meant."

"But those are my terms. I'm a gentleman, but I have my limits."

"Can they start tomorrow?" Sinai wiggled in the blankets before producing a pair of black lace panties. Dom could only assume she had been wearing under her nightshirt.

"Give me one night of full access, and you have a deal," he said.

Sinai nodded and flung the sheets off of her body. Dom wasted no time bringing her legs up to his shoulders and burying his face into her core. She cried out and gripped his head, guiding his rhythm against her exposed flesh.

"I'm going to make tonight unforgettable," he growled into her pussy.

7

A YEAR LATER, VALENTINE'S DAY...

Sinai sat across from Dom at Café Yarrow. They usually weren't open this late, but Dom had pulled some strings and more than likely opened his pocketbook. The owner herself was both cook and server for the evening.

"I can't believe you rented out this place on Valentine's Day! We could have just ordered to go and spent the night at home," Sinai whispered.

She didn't need to whisper, they were the only ones in the restaurant, but she hadn't wanted the owner to overhear and get offended. The woman had an inhuman hearing ability. Something Sinai had learned the hard way when she'd complained about mushrooms on her plate last month, and the woman herself had come to chew her out for being picky as a child.

"It's symbolic," Dom whispered back.

"Symbolic of what?"

Dom smiled. "The first time I realized my feelings for you were more than just unmitigated lust. No way in hell I would have sat a whole hour waiting on a woman I only wanted to get in bed with."

Sinai giggled. "Seriously, Dom!"

"Oh, I'm very serious. Speaking of which," Dom placed a blue velvet ring box on the table.

Sinai froze and stared at him, opened mouthed. "Dom, that isn't what I think it is, is it?"

"Just open it."

Sinai reached for the box timidly. The past year had been a rollercoaster for both of them. The whole no-sex rule had never made it into effect after that very unforgettable first night. Still, they'd managed to balance a healthy friendship with their sexual exploits. But, their relationship status hadn't progressed much further than "it's complicated."

Sinai opened the box but was afraid to look. Afraid that there was a giant rock with the L word and forever attached to it. Dom laughed and snatched the box back from her. He took her hand in his and slid the ring on her right hand.

"Sinai Carlisle, will you be my girlfriend?"

Now it was Sinai's turn to laugh. "Oh my God, Dom! That's it, A promise ring?"

"What? You don't like it? I can take it back."

Sinai snatched her hand away before he could slip the ring off her finger. "Yes! Yes, I'll be your girlfriend."

Sinai leaned forward to kiss Dom but suddenly, there was a wooden spatula between them. They looked up to see the owner of the restaurant scowling at the two of them.

"Girlfriend? You had me close my restaurant on the busiest night of the year to ask her to be your girlfriend? Boy, if you don't get on your knees and propose, I'm banning you both from here forever."

She turned and started walking away, muttering under

her breath. "Young fools don't even know what love is. Fated mates playing dumb."

Sinai looked down at the ring on her finger and back at Dom.

"Don't you dare."

"What, you don't want to marry me?" He feigned hurt.

"Not if your only reason is that you'll miss your favorite place to eat grits."

Dom slid from his chair and knelt down beside her.

"Sinai, will you promise to say yes when I ask you to marry me at a later date, not because I was threatened with losing my favorite grits spot?"

Sinai nearly fell out of her chair laughing so hard.

"Yes, Dom. I promise."

Dom swept her into his arms and kissed her before turning to the kitchen.

"She said yes!" he called out.

"Y'all children play too much," the owner responded.

Sinai tugged on Dom's shirt and kissed him again. They had plenty of time to figure out the whole marriage thing. For now, she would enjoy their promise of a future no matter how it turned out.

About The Author

Author Stella Williams

Stella Williams is a Blogger and USA TODAY Bestselling Paranormal Romance & Urban Fantasy Author who lives in Washington State. She has a degree in Anthropology from The University of California, Santa Cruz. Stella prides herself in using her studies to create diverse worlds and characters for her novels. You can find more about Stella Williams on her website: www.serpentinecreative.com

Keep up to date with Stella and her latest projects.
https://serpentinecreative.com/getsocial/

Want More of Stella's Seductive Supernatural World? Explore Stella's Catalogue
https://serpentinecreative.com/getbooks

Continue reading for an excerpt of

Ferocious
Secret of Ceres Book 1

Full Moon

Daphne climbed from her bedroom window and onto the landing of the fire escape. She paused as it creaked under her weight. She started sneaking out three months ago and knew it would hold her weight, just not how long.

The apartment building where she and her family lived survived on sheer will alone. The elevators hardly ever worked, the stairwell reeked of urine and weed smoke. No one cared what anyone around them did. Everyone stuck to themselves regardless of the situation. The perfect environment outside of Ceres for a family of Aura to go unnoticed. The easiest place to hide from the outside world while still living and navigating within it.

Her family could afford better. Fear and proximity to Ceres kept them stuck in this hell hole. Daphne dreamed of living without fear. Lots of Aura teens who grew up outside of the Great Sanctuary of Ceres felt the way she did. They didn't want to choose between the freedom of the outside world and the freedom to use their gifts. They wanted both. On nights like this, they defied the rules by gathering to practice their energy knowledge without limitation. The Resistance, they called themselves, organized and fought for the freedom to be themselves. At least from what the brochure said. Daphne found The Resistance mostly blogged about social injustices around the world and partied at the local hot spot, Club Obelisk.

The full moon beckoned, filling her with excited energy. Daphne rushed down the metal ladder using her Aura energy to sense the way in the pitch black of the alleyway. The buildings stood tall enough to block any of the moon's magnificent light from reaching its secrets. The only other source of light in the alley had long been broken, and no one cared to fix it.

"Took you long enough," James said, startling Daphne.

She smiled and launched herself into his waiting arms. Daphne and James flirted for a month now, and she hoped that maybe this evening made things official.

"Benji wouldn't fall asleep. I had to wait him out," Daphne whispered.

He took her mouth in a passionate kiss. They made out in the dark until a sharp whistle cut through the silent night air, time to go. The others wouldn't wait for them much longer. James took Daphne's hand and led her out of the alley to a waiting van. Tonight, was a special night. They wouldn't be joining The Resistance at Club Obelisk. It was their first official date—a house party being thrown somewhere on the outskirts of town. While Daphne preferred that they travel to the party just the two of them, she couldn't be any more excited.

"Hurry up. They are waiting," the driver said.

He looked back at them through the rearview mirror. Daphne never met these boys before. Human, but not part of The Resistance. She knew all ten of the human members there, James included. It made Daphne nervous. She studied James' energy. Finding him to be calm and excited, she snuggled closer to him.

"Let's go, then. Wouldn't want to keep them waiting," James said.

His voice sounded deeper than usual. Like he wanted to project a manly façade in front of his friends.

"Who's all going to be there? Will there be anyone I know," Daphne asked.

James smiled at her and shook his head.

"No one you know. I want you to get to know a different set of friends.

I'm sure once you meet them, you'll understand," James said.

Daphne ignored the warning bells going off in her head. James acted like a different person, but that's what humans did. They changed personalities based on the situation. Daphne could understand that, living her life as an Aura in the outside world. Still, Daphne couldn't shake the gnawing feeling in her stomach.

She shifted in her seat. Her senses picked up on a delicate swirl of dark energy. They drove farther and farther from the city. Her palms began to sweat, and her stomach started to twist in knot—the air heavy with ill intent.

"Pull over!" Daphne snapped as they reached the last few blocks of civilization.

James' friends chuckled, and he wrapped a tight arm around her waist.

"Chill out, babe. We've got big plans for you tonight."

The implication of his words sent Daphne into a panic. She focused on the vehicle's engine, feeling out its energy until she found just the right component to manipulate. The car sputtered and began to smoke before the engine died. As soon as it slowed, Daphne lunged for the door. She almost made it out van before James grabbed her by the ankles.

"I thought I told you to neutralize her before she got in the van," the driver shouted.

She struggled with all her might.

"I did! I slipped her the potion while we kissed," James snapped.

Daphne screamed and kicked for dear life as they pulled her back into the van. She prayed for someone, anyone to hear and come to her rescue. She missed her chance.

"Guess I'll do it the old-fashioned way. Boss is going to be pissed," the other boy from the van said.

A big black object came flying at Daphne's face. The force of someone's fist impacting her jaw sent her flying into the wall of the van. She heard the sickening sound of flesh connecting with flesh before her head hit the metal behind her. Everything went black.

Ferocious

A Steamy & Suspenseful Paranormal Romance

Available Now

www.serpentinecreative.com/getbooks